Mack inhaled sharply as an ugly thought began to dawn

"You were snooping around this afternoon, deliberately creating drama, which you knew would get back to me eventually, because you were ticked I wasn't giving you my full attention. Maybe you thought you could find something you could use as—I hesitate to use the word *blackmail*—leverage?"

Chloe stuck her finger in the center of his chest. And pushed. "I'm not that kind of person. I was simply doing my job as best I could—alone—once it became evident you weren't taking my assignment seriously. An assignment, I might remind you, your boss requested."

When it looked as if she might poke him again, he took a step backward. "Lady, don't try to throw your weight around. I'm bigger than you by a good hundred pounds."

Chloe's cheeks flamed red, making the freckles across her nose stand out. She pulled herself erect. "I'm not going away, Deputy Whittaker. I'm staying right here in town...."

Dear Reader,

This was a difficult story to write. Quite frankly, my personal life has been in turmoil for the past year. I'd get up every day and face the computer screen, wondering if I could help my hero and heroine with their lives when I was having such a difficult time with my own.

Deputy Sheriff Mack Whittaker is guilt ridden over an event in his past. His reaction is to shut down emotionally and throw himself into his job. Reporter Chloe Atherton harbors her own traumatic touchstone, but she feels confident that by pursuing the truth in the form of facts, she has her life under control. At one point in writing I found myself yelling at the computer screen, "Wake up! Control is merely an illusion!" Harsh. Even if you're yelling at fictional characters.

So...if I wasn't going to give these two the comfort of control, what was left to them? (And to me. Because, if you haven't yet guessed, I was kinda countin' on Mack and Chloe leading me out of my own personal wilderness.) The answer was as it always is: We survive—and thrive—by first opening our hearts.

As I helped my hero and heroine grasp that particular lifeline, I pulled myself to safety, as well.

Now I wish you love,

Amy Frazier

FALLING FOR THE DEPUTY
Amy Frazier

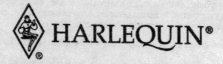

HARLEQUIN®

TORONTO • NEW YORK • LONDON
AMSTERDAM • PARIS • SYDNEY • HAMBURG
STOCKHOLM • ATHENS • TOKYO • MILAN • MADRID
PRAGUE • WARSAW • BUDAPEST • AUCKLAND

ISBN-13: 978-0-373-71495-7
ISBN-10:   0-373-71495-5

FALLING FOR THE DEPUTY

www.eHarlequin.com

Printed in U.S.A.

ABOUT THE AUTHOR

Having worked at various times as a teacher, a media specialist, a professional storyteller and a freelance artist, Amy Frazier now writes full-time. She lives in Georgia with her husband, two philosophical cats and one very rascally terrier-mix dog.

Books by Amy Frazier

HARLEQUIN SUPERROMANCE

1269–THE TRICK TO GETTING A MOM
1298–INDEPENDENCE DAY
1423–BLAME IT ON THE DOG
1456–COMFORT AND JOY
1473–SINGLE-DAD SHERIFF

SILHOUETTE ROMANCE

1347–FAMILY BY THE BUNCH

SILHOUETTE SPECIAL EDITION

 954–THE SECRET BABY
1030–NEW BRIDE IN TOWN
1036–WAITING AT THE ALTAR
1043–A GOOD GROOM IS HARD TO FIND
1188–BABY STARTS THE WEDDING MARCH
1270–CELEBRATE THE CHILD
1354–A BUNDLE OF MIRACLES

CHAPTER ONE

THE TOP OF HIS HEAD was about to blow.

His mother had just called him—for the third time this morning—to ask if the reporter from the *Western Carolina Sun* had arrived in Applegate yet.

No.

Thank God.

Undeterred by his increasingly testy responses, Lily had insisted Mack bring the man or woman to supper at the farmhouse one night this week. For a nice down-home mix of business and pleasure, she'd said. That wasn't going to happen. People, his mother chief among them, thought because Mack had joined AA and was back on the force, he was ready to rejoin the human race.

He wasn't.

He still struggled to stay sober. Doing his job helped. Period.

To that end, Mack pulled his sheriff's department cruiser to the side of the road behind a battered Yugo. He cast a glance over the wreck of a car. Primer paint in several hues covered all but one fender. The driver's-side taillight was broken. Bumper stickers, some faded beyond legibility, littered the car's sorry backside. Two caught his attention. *The facts will set you free* and *Pray for peace; work for justice.* Call him cynical, but it wasn't that easy.

At first he'd thought the car was abandoned. It wasn't unusual in the mountains, valleys and hollows of Colum County, North Carolina, to find stolen cars stripped and ditched by the side of an out-of-the-way road. But this Yugo—Mack doubted it would have appealed to a thief even in its heyday—had a current registration sticker on the plate. From his cruiser, he began a computer check.

As the door of the Yugo opened and the driver got out, Mack stopped mid-routine. Despite the glare of the midday sun, he instinctively ran a visual of the slender woman, who shaded her eyes with one hand. In the other she clutched a crumpled road map. She wore a button-up sweater that looked as if it had shrunk during washing, a faded ankle-length dress that had "church rummage sale" written all over it and black lace-up boots, the kind his great-granny used to wear. When she finally took her hand from her eyes, Mack saw she was young. And pretty.

He stepped out of the cruiser and approached her. "Can I help you?"

She smiled, and her fresh face framed by tousled strawberry-blond hair, made him think she'd never been disappointed in her entire life. "Is this the road to Applegate?"

"One of them." He gave her car's interior a cursory inspection. Books, notebooks and loose papers filled the back seat. She was probably a student at the college over in Brevard, although she looked too young to be even a freshman.

"One of them? Is that local humor?" Cocking her head to the side, she gazed directly at him. Mack blinked and discovered the proverbial shoe on the other foot. Usually he was the one who made other people uncomfortable because of his size and uniform.

But his presence didn't faze this young woman in the least. She stood almost toe-to-toe with him, so close he could see a dusting of freckles across her nose, and waited patiently, with an air of innocence he found disconcerting.

He scowled. "Humor? No. I'm told I don't have an ounce left in me." To prove the point, he added, "Do you know your car has a broken taillight?"

"You should see the other guy." She grinned wickedly, revealing perfect teeth. "Humor," she explained.

"It's not a laughing matter. I could write you up—"

"Oh, please, don't," she said as she might say no, thank you to a second helping of cake. "When I get to Applegate, I'll get it fixed."

Kids. Not a care in the world. Making it on looks

and youth alone. Mack felt a jolt of envy. After what he'd seen and done half a world away, carefree would never be a mood ascribed to him again.

He ran his fingers over the broken plastic of the Yugo's taillight. "See that you get this fixed. Take it to Mel's on Main Street." He turned to go. "And afterward, come to the sheriff's office with the receipt. To show me you kept your word."

"Yes, sir. If nothing else, I'm a woman of my word."

Was he mistaken or was there a hint of sass under the show of respect? He looked back at her. Her gray eyes revealed nothing but a clear, ingenuous light. A kid. That was what she was. A wet-behind-the-ears kid cut loose from her mama's apron strings.

"And I should ask for whom?" She squinted at his name tag, sounding suspiciously defiant.

"Deputy Sheriff Whittaker." Without wasting any more time, he walked back to his patrol car.

"Deputy Whittaker?" Her voice, clear, high and musical, sailed through the air like birdsong on the spring breeze.

Reluctantly he turned to look at her again. "Yes?"

"You said this was one of the roads to Applegate, but am I headed in the right direction?"

Had he ever, even as a boy, exuded such a wide-eyed innocence?

"You're…you're headed in the right direction." He took a step backward and bumped into his car's grille. When she winced, he added hastily, "You can't miss Mel's repair shop. Right next to the county courthouse."

She fluttered her fingers next to her head, a half-wave, half-salute that made him think she might be mocking him.

Settling behind the wheel of the cruiser, he waited for her to be on her way. That was his excuse. Actually he'd have liked to sit on the side of the road indefinitely. Do nothing more than watch the wrens gather materials for their nests. But in an hour he had an appointment back at headquarters with that reporter from the *Sun*.

Another reason for the headache that originated at the base of his skull and pounded a path to his temples.

In a PR move to show the county residents how far the newly rehabilitated department had come, Sheriff Garrett McQuire had requested the newspaper interview. Mack saw the need. His boss and longtime buddy had worked ceaselessly, cleaning up the mess the former sheriff Easley and his cronies had left behind. What Mack hadn't foreseen was that Garrett would take off on his honeymoon and leave Mack with the reporter. He suspected the sheriff saw the handover of responsibilities as part of his deputy's personal rehabilitation. If Mack didn't owe Garrett so much—both as a boss and as a buddy, he would've rescheduled.

Instead, he put the patrol car in gear and headed

back to town. If he was going through with this, he needed to be the first on-site for the appointment. He didn't need a member of the press waiting, unsupervised.

THE YUGO BUCKED IN complaint as Chloe drove in second gear down Applegate's Main Street. Squinting against the sunlight, she searched for Mel's repair shop. Ah, there was the domed courthouse and, in its shadow, a two-bay cinder block garage with kudzu creeping up one side. She parked in front, then pulled on the stubborn emergency brake. Reaching into the back seat, she grabbed a pad of paper to jot down a few notes and capture her first impression of Deputy Whittaker.

Thirty-something, he was handsome—the uniform automatically did that for a guy. Strong jaw. A nose that could have been considered classically Roman if the deputy hadn't broken it. An old sports injury? From the barred and bolted look in Whittaker's dark brown eyes, Chloe had an instinctive feeling he'd reveal nothing he didn't want known. Either about his job or himself. If she had anything to do with him this week, he might prove problematic. A difficult lock resisting the pick.

The Colum County Sheriff's Department. Now there lay a potentially rewarding project. Her first feature story. Her first byline. A tiny shiver ran through her as she anticipated the opportunity. Hastily she wrote, "Deputy Whittaker. Humorless.

Stickler for details," before tossing the notepad onto the passenger seat.

She wrestled with the door of the Yugo. "Honestly, you are one more act of resistance away from the scrap heap," she warned the mutinous vehicle when she managed to break free. She kicked the door shut behind her.

At the garage's first bay, she gingerly stepped around a pick up to approach the bottom half of a coverall-clad mechanic leaning well under the truck's raised hood.

"Mr. Mel?" she inquired with well-practiced Southern deference. "Deputy Whittaker sent me."

"Mr. Mel! Now that's a hoot!" The top half of the technician popped into view.

Chloe immediately recognized her error.

The person in the coveralls would never be mistaken for a man. She had wild red hair caught up in a bandanna, a movie-star smile and classically feminine features, not to mention a voluptuous body. But the woman's voice belonged to the racetrack pit or smoke-filled juke joints. Chloe didn't even hazard a guess at her age.

The mechanic stuck her greasy hands on her hips. "So the deputy sent you over to see Mr. Mel. Maybe his sense of humor's finally coming back."

"It was my mistake. He said to pull into Mel's auto repair. I jumped to conclusions. Sorry. That's not my style."

"Well, I'm Mel. Short for Melody. My mama was hoping for a girlie-girl." She rolled her big blue eyes. "But grease monkeys defy gender, honey. Come on in the office. I'm due a break." She wiped her hands on a rag.

Chloe followed the woman into a cramped room no bigger than a utility closet.

"Coffee?" Mel raised a half-full pot from the automatic coffeemaker perched on a packing crate. "Nectar of the goddess."

"Please."

"You're new in town." The woman handed Chloe a mug of sludge-black liquid.

"I'm a newspaper reporter for the *Western Carolina Sun*," she replied, taking a sip of the bitter brew and noting the three-year-old SPCA calendar hanging on the wall.

"A reporter?" Mel paused, coffeepot in midair. The energy in the room shifted from positive to unnervingly negative.

"Sheriff McQuire suggested we do an article on his revamped department," Chloe explained, trying to establish credibility. "I have my first interview with him in a few minutes."

"That'll be difficult, seeing as he's on his honeymoon." Mel's chuckle swelled to a roar. She slapped her thigh, spilling coffee on the cracked linoleum floor. "I bet he did that deliberately."

Chloe clenched her mug in both hands, hoping the

heat would defuse her rising irritation. "And the reason would be?"

"Even though, as sheriff, Garrett would recognize the need for positive PR, personally, he and journalists aren't on the best of terms after they hounded his wife." Mel thumped the pot back on the coffeemaker's heating ring. "Made the whole town miserable. You'd have to be living under a rock not to know about it."

Okay. The runaway heiress. But… "I wasn't part of that feeding frenzy." No, she'd been stuck on the garden-club beat.

Mel raised one eyebrow.

"So—" in the face of this woman's disbelief, Chloe forged ahead "—who's left to handle my interview?"

"While Garrett's gone, Mack's in charge."

"Mack?"

"Deputy Whittaker."

Interesting. The lock in need of a pick.

"The guy who sent you here for…what?" Mel prodded.

"Yes. My car's broken taillight. The deputy ran into me outside town. Didn't cite me on condition I see you."

"I gotta say this new department's been good for my business."

"Do you have an arrangement?" Chloe blurted out. She fumbled in her pocket for her notepad, then realized she'd left it in the Yugo. She'd heard of small

towns adding to their coffers with overzealous tick-
eting or costly kick-back repairs that targeted motor-
ists passing through.

Mel dropped a rag on the spilled coffee. As she
bent over to wipe it up, she uttered a terse no. When
she stood again, the sparkle had gone from her eyes.
"I merely meant this particular crew adheres strictly
to the law."

"So what's Deputy Whittaker like?" Chloe asked,
struggling to reconnect.

Mel tossed the coffee-soaked rag into a bin by the
door. "Let's look at that taillight," she said, all
business now.

If this was the level of Applegate respect, cooperation and disclosure that Chloe could expect, she
had her work cut out for her.

MACK LEFT THE DOOR to the sheriff's office open. A
symbolic gesture. Let the reporter see the department had nothing whatsoever to hide.

He placed his Stetson on a rack behind the door,
then sat on the edge of the desk, feeling edgy
himself. His headache had subsided to a dull throb.
He relished the law-and-order part of his job, not the
public relations. He examined his watch. Twice.

Garrett and he had talked about how they wanted
the new Colum County Sheriff's Department's story
told. To that end, they'd hoped to get a reporter without
an agenda, who'd write an unbiased story that would

accurately portray both the danger and the drudgery of rural law enforcement. They'd agreed the article shouldn't be about individuals, but about the team.

Thinking about the fishbowl position he was now in, Mack's muscles went rigid. The pencil he gripped snapped in two.

"Surely, the prospect of meeting with me can't generate that much tension."

He jerked his head up to see the young woman who drove the battered Yugo, standing in the office doorway, carrying an enormous backpack. He chucked the ruined pencil in the trash, then stood. "Did you get your car fixed?"

"Mel says I can pick it up this afternoon before she closes."

"Is that going to throw your schedule off?" He didn't really want to know. He was trying to be… human. Approachable. Practicing for that reporter. "Work? School?"

"No." The kid stepped into the room. "I was planning to stay the week, anyway. At June Parker's bed and breakfast. While I take care of my assignment."

"Let me guess. Appalachian folkways." The professors at Brevard College often sent their students to do field work in Colum County.

"No. I've come to see you. Well, Sheriff McQuire, but I understand you're the one in charge at the moment."

"I am. What can I do for you?"

She extended her hand. "I'm Chloe Atherton. Reporter for the *Western Carolina Sun*. I have an appointment."

He inhaled sharply. *My head.* Ignoring her outstretched hand, Mack walked around the desk and glared at the sheriff's calendar. He deliberately placed the tips of his fingers on Garrett's illegible handwriting next to today's date. Gave himself a couple of seconds to absorb it.

This kid was the reporter?

"You could have told me who you were back by the roadside," he said at last, looking up.

"You could have told me Mel was a woman." She plunked her battered backpack on the floor, then perched on the chair opposite his desk. "Can we begin?" Without waiting for his reply, she pulled various items from the backpack.

He remained standing, the desk solidly between them. "Ms. Atherton, how long have you been a newspaper reporter?"

"I think I'm the one doing the interviewing." There was a defiant tilt to her chin. "But if it will make you feel more comfortable…no, I'm not thirteen years old."

He'd been thinking more like seventeen.

"I'm twenty-six," she offered, lining up a notebook, a pencil, a small tape recorder and what appeared to be an expensive Nikon camera on the metal desk. As if the space were hers to do with as she pleased. "How old are you?"

He frowned. "Do you need to know?"

"My newspaper still requires ages."

"Thirty-five," he said, suddenly feeling ten years older. "But this article isn't supposed to be about me."

"Maybe not, but you're my first interview."

Damn. Although she looked like a teenager, she handled herself with the equanimity of a pro.

"I can give you an hour today," he allowed. "We can use the time to work up a schedule for the rest of the week."

"Only an hour? I'd hoped—"

He raised his hand to cut her off. "Can that car of yours withstand a week's worth of cruising these roads?"

"I intend to ride with you."

He rubbed his forehead as the headache came roaring out of retirement. "I don't think so."

"Deputy Whittaker, this article was Sheriff McQuire's idea. He contacted my paper. He suggested a human-interest story on a week in the life of a sheriff's department. I wouldn't get much of an idea of what the job entailed if I were to follow several car lengths behind you, would I?"

"I doubt Garrett—Sheriff McQuire—had a ride-along in mind. Liability issues—"

She flipped through her notebook. "I've done my homework. Ah, here it is. Sheriff McQuire encourages public-safety interns from the college. They ride in the cruisers. I'll ride in the cruiser."

"He didn't tell me—"

"Call him."

"He's on his honeymoon."

Victorious, she dropped the notebook in her lap, crossed her arms and leaned back in her chair. "Then it's settled. You'll have to take my word for it. I've already kept my word once by having that taillight fixed."

She wasn't riding with him. He wouldn't argue now, but he'd sure as tomorrow think of some excuse not to have this reporter dogging his every move. Hell, he'd only recently begun talking to his fellow deputies. Had Garrett really planned this? Could Mack get someone in the county health department to sanction the sheriff for practicing psychology without a license?

"Now…" She was scribbling something on her notepad. "One way we might approach the article is from the perspective of the evolution of a rural office. I noticed a huge vacation community—Ryder's Ridge?—as I was entering town. And another new year-round subdivision closer to town. Surely progress, if you want to call it that, has changed the complexion of the county. Changed your job."

Putting aside for a moment the problem of her riding with him, he stared hard at her. It had taken her only a few minutes to get to the root of the department's problems. Sheriff Easley hadn't been able or willing to move into the twenty-first century. Of course, the problem was more complicated than what she'd picked up on, but she'd come very close to the mark. Not too shabby for a green reporter.

"Deputy Whittaker? How's my assessment?"

"Rapid growth is a major issue," he grudgingly replied.

She wrote something down. "I have an idea about the who, the what, the where and the when. Now all I need is the why." She licked the tip of her pencil. "Why did Sheriff McQuire call in the media? Is this an election year? Does he need to look good in the polls?"

Mack didn't like questions that began innocuously but packed a hidden sting. "Sheriff McQuire wants you to write about the department. Not about him. Not about me. Not about any of the other deputies. Not as individuals, but as a team. Doing what we're supposed to do. Our job is to protect and serve."

He came around the desk, then leaned forward until his face was within inches of hers. "Now, let me ask *you* a few questions. Do you have something to prove? Is this assignment a stepping-stone to bigger and better assignments? Would your boss be happier with solid reporting or with some trumped-up exposé?"

Chloe reacted to his deliberate intimidation by inhaling sharply and sitting back in her seat until her spine pressed against the hard molded plastic. What had lit a fire under Deputy Whittaker? Did he interact with all reporters this way, or did he have a problem with female reporters specifically? She made a mental note to find out the number of women in the department and how they were treated.

"Let me rephrase the question," she replied. She'd get to any prejudices he might have later. When she caught him in an unguarded moment. "Why would the sheriff want an outsider poking about the department? Why not issue a press release? In any event, why do you think your day-to-day operations would be of interest to the general public?"

"Why would the public be interested in how we run the department?" he asked, his expression growing darker. "Did you skip your junior-high classes on local government?"

"No. I happen to have loved—"

"Let me spell it out for you." The muscles in his jaw twitched as he leaned back against the desk. "The history of this office—this public-safety office—goes back to England and the days of Robin Hood. The sheriff's an elected official, the highest law-enforcement official in the county. Entrusted with keeping the peace."

"The point being?" It was her turn to bridle. She'd never liked lectures. And she didn't like overbearing men.

"The point..." He tapped her notepad with his index finger. "If the electorate has the sense they were born with, they better damn well want to know how we're carrying out our duties." As his voice rose, he accidentally knocked a stack of file folders off a tall cabinet onto the floor. He ignored the mess.

Heavens. If this was the deputy in charge, what was the sheriff like? Chloe refused to be daunted. If the truth be told, his civic ardor excited her. Electrified the room. What good was a career if you weren't passionate about it?

She crossed her legs, sat up straight and met the deputy's fierce expression. His eyes weren't merely dark brown, they were hickory-nut-brown, she noticed. And hard. "Then we'd better back up. The sheriff said y'all had turned the office around. What was the problem?"

He remained immobile for several moments, staring at her. The information had to be public record. Narrowing his eyes, he appeared to come to a decision.

"Five years ago," he began with great deliberation, "Zach Taylor sold four hundred acres of prime land to a real-estate developer who, in turn, built two complexes—year-round executive homes and expensive vacation homes. Those complexes attracted hundreds of families to Applegate. The population of Colum County soared."

"Bringing new problems to your department."

"It wasn't our—Sheriff McQuire's—department at the time."

"But there were problems."

"Yes. But I think Sheriff McQuire intended that you concentrate on the present, not the past."

That wasn't how the media worked, but she knew to choose her battles. "How have things changed?" She tuned into his body language as she waited.

He began to pace the cramped quarters, stepping over the spilled folders. "For one thing, we now run things strictly by the book."

Chloe took down his words without comment. There would be time enough to determine if the new sheriff ran an honest department. *Believe only what you see, what you can prove,* her mother, a scientist, always said.

She raised her head. "And for another?"

"For another, we've brought the department into the computer age."

Suppressing an urge to yawn, she bet her next paycheck her readers couldn't care less about the sheriff's computers. But the personnel might be a different issue. Take this particular deputy, for instance. Confrontational. Ardent. Protective. But what, exactly, was he protecting? She'd find out soon enough.

"What about the sheriff's staff?" she asked.

"What about us?"

"What makes you different from the last batch?"

He flinched. "We're handpicked—"

"Not elected like the sheriff?"

"No, but—"

"Mack!" Another deputy stuck her head through the office doorway. "You're wanted at the high school. Stat."

As Deputy Whittaker reached for his Stetson, Chloe stuffed her pencil, notebook and camera in her backpack, then activated her pocket tape recorder. When the two deputies left, Chloe trotted along right behind, observing every move, picking up every word.

"What's the story?" Whittaker asked.

"Rival groups again," the second deputy answered. Her name tag read Breckinridge. "Same old beef. This time someone pulled a knife."

"Do we have anyone out there?"

"McMillan and Sooner answered the call. The kids are being held in the school cafeteria until you and the parents get there. Most of them are from The Program. That's why Principal Cox called for you."

Chloe didn't understand everything they were saying. She hoped the recorder was picking it up, allowing her to get clarification later. This was the kind of eye-witness involvement she'd anticipated, the kind that would lead to a compelling story. Her pulse raced.

Deputy Breckinridge halted at the big double doors leading to the parking lot, but Chloe slipped outside behind Whittaker. He didn't acknowledge her presence.

When he got to his cruiser, she automatically went to the passenger door.

"What the hell do you think you're doing?" he barked across the roof.

"I'm working my story."

"Today's interview is finished." Abruptly he got into the driver's side and slammed the door. She opened the passenger door and climbed in, slamming her door for good measure.

"Get out." By his tone of voice, he meant business.

So did she. "Drive."

He glared at her.

"While you're driving," she added, "you can explain the history of this altercation."

Muttering under his breath, he turned the key in the ignition. As he pulled the patrol car out of the parking lot, she could feel the anger radiating off him.

"I'm not going to waste time arguing with you." The veins corded and pulsed along his temple. "When we get back, though, I'm calling the *Sun* to request your replacement."

He wouldn't dare. But in case he did, she hunkered down in her seat and prepared to defend her right to be there.

CHAPTER TWO

IT WAS ALL MACK COULD DO not to speed. At least Deputies Sooner and McMillan had this call under control. The kid—the reporter—wouldn't be in any danger. Only in the way.

When he heard a click, he looked over at her. She had taken his picture. An itchy heat crawled up the back of his neck to join forces with the headache. "Put that thing away," he warned, holding up his hand to shield himself.

"You'd better get used to it. Do you know how many photos I'll have to take to get two or three perfect ones for the article?"

He grasped the steering wheel tightly and concentrated on the double yellow line in front of him. On the evergreens and granite boulders crowding the edges of the two-lane county road. On anything but her. She was an invasion.

"Put it away for this call," he ground out. "Even under the best of circumstances, you'd have to get written releases to photograph the students. And these aren't the best of circumstances."

"But I'm photographing you—"

"Put it away."

She sighed.

He refused to look at her again.

After several seconds he could hear her zip the camera into her backpack. "Why were you called to the school," she asked, her words measured, "if your deputies already had the situation in hand?"

He took a deep breath. "This program's the sheriff's baby. Right now, I'm acting sheriff."

"What program?"

He might as well tell her the whole story. She wasn't going to let up until she got it. "Because of county-wide growth," he began, "we had to build a third high school. Letting the seniors spend their last year at their two old schools—McEaster and North Colum—the board of ed pulled surplus juniors and underclassmen from the overcrowded schools to attend the new one—Harriman."

"And if this area is anything like all the others in the South," Chloe said, "high-school sports rule. They fuel small-town social life and loyalties." She was quick to catch on.

"Yeah." He ran his window down. Quick to catch on or not, she made the car's interior feel too close for comfort. "The underclassmen have settled in fine, but the juniors have the hardest time forgetting. McEaster and North Colum used to be fierce rivals. Now the students from those two schools are expected to pull together for a brand-new school."

"Deputy Breckinridge said someone pulled a knife this time. That's extreme." She had good ears, too.

"You have to understand. Not only are we dealing with the displacement of old school loyalties, but also with an influx of newcomers, mostly affluent families from the city. Plus immigrant workers who've come to service an expanding vacation sector. There's cultural friction...and more. We may be rural, but we aren't untouched by drugs. Meth has replaced moonshine."

"And you can never minimize the pressure of teenage hormones."

Caught off guard by the thoughtfulness in her tone of voice, he hazarded a sideways look at her. "You've got it." Her eyes half closed, she was contemplating him. He snapped his head forward. "So...Sheriff McQuire established a program," he said, retreating to his spiel. "A public-safety program that's an offshoot of the Junior Deputy Program we run in the elementary schools. The sheriff put me in charge of the high school."

"I can't picture teenagers willingly participating in something called a Junior Deputy Program."

The cruiser's two-way radio crackled. As she reached out to adjust the volume, he put out his hand to stop her. Apparently, she wasn't real good with boundaries.

"At the high-school level," he explained, "we just call it The Program. And it's as no-nonsense as its name. We deal with peer pressure, drugs, conflict resolution. All under the umbrella of public safety. We pull no punches in how we talk to the kids."

Straining against her seat belt, she leaned forward to examine the controls on the dashboard. "Why did Sheriff McQuire put you in charge of it?"

Probably because Mack knew these kids inside out. He'd been one of them. Full of piss and vinegar, his grandmother used to say. But he wasn't about to tell this to a stranger, a reporter, no less. "You'd have to ask the sheriff."

He could feel her eyes on him, but he kept his own on the road. "Back to the kids," she said, her tone level. Patient, even. When you didn't look at her, she came off as mature. "Even with a realistic course for them, they still get in trouble?"

"They're kids. Obviously you don't have any." Out of the corner of his eye, he thought he saw her stiffen.

"N-no." Her hesitation seemed out of character. "I've never been married. Are you married?" She lobbed that question as she might something dangerous she wanted to get rid of. "For the record."

"Married to the job. But this article's not about me, remember."

Did he hear an *oh, yeah?* in the silence?

"So what's the game plan when we reach the high school?" she finally asked.

"By the time we get there, the principal should have assembled the parents—even the working parents. Getting them involved in school altercations should cut down on more serious…incidents in the future. I'm essentially going to run a conflict-resolution session with these kids, their parents and the school counselors."

"And me?"

With relief he saw the cell-phone tower above the trees of the high-school campus. The school itself couldn't appear fast enough for him. He needed to get back to his duties. Clear-cut action to solve a specific problem. And away from all this hopscotch questioning.

"And you? You're going to sit in the corner," he replied, suspecting he might later regret this decision. "Out of the way. Where you'll observe and take notes."

"Why should I take notes? I thought when we got back to your office, you were going to call the *Sun* and get them to replace me."

As if it required all his attention, he hit the directional signal as they neared the school entrance. Made himself listen to it click three times before answering her. "Let's say you're quick," he admitted. "You catch on to what's happening without me hammering it home. If you stay out of my way and let me do my job, maybe we can work something out."

"Maybe? Am I, like, on parole?"

Was she trying to tick him off? He pulled into the parking lot and stopped in front of the main entrance. With an irritated shove, he opened his door and got out.

CHLOE OBSERVED THE STUDENTS, their parents and school officials as they dispersed from the cafeteria. She'd been witness to Deputy Whittaker's impressive display of self-control balanced by his uncanny understanding of human nature.

Surprise, surprise. The man had a non-prickly side to him.

It was good he'd been the focus of her story because, once inside the school, surrounded by teenagers, she'd remembered why she'd told her editor she'd never do the board of education beat. Claire would have been seventeen…

Fortunately the deputy interrupted her reverie as he walked across the big room to where she sat on a folding chair next to the emergency exit. He should be pleased he'd brought the intervention to such a positive end, yet he didn't look it. His shoulders were stiff, his mouth was set in a severe line, and he carried himself with military bearing.

Automatically Chloe rose and retreated a step toward the emergency door. Why was it that in his presence she felt compelled to stand and salute?

"Ready to go?" His staccato words jolted her. Her backside hit the door's push bar and the door opened. The alarm sounded. The other deputies, the principal, the school counselors, several remaining parents and their kids froze. The kids began to snicker.

Whittaker reached past her with a grimace that said she'd lost any Brownie points she'd scored during the meeting by staying out of the way. Wordlessly he disengaged the alarm, then closed the door.

"Reporter humor?" he asked.

When she chose to consider that a rhetorical question and remained silent, he grasped her by the elbow and propelled her out of the cafeteria.

"Tomorrow I think I'll hand you over to Deputy Breckinridge," he said as he marched her through the school corridors to the front door. "She's on desk duty."

Feeling like a truant on the way to the principal's office, Chloe tried not to pant keeping up with his long-legged stride. "I don't think desk duty was what Sheriff McQuire had in mind when he called in the press," she declared, wresting control of her elbow from Whittaker. "Besides, you and I haven't finished with today."

In the parking lot he swiveled to face her. "I'm in charge while the sheriff's away. Today's interview is finished. I'll drive you back to the B and B."

Her mouth dropped open. "Now wait a minute. This isn't going to work as a piecemeal deal. I'm supposed to walk in your shoes. Get a feel for your job. A couple hours a day won't cut it. You haven't even offered me a doughnut."

Instantly she regretted her unprofessional dig.

He slid behind the wheel. Because she didn't doubt he'd leave her in the parking lot, she scrambled into the passenger seat.

The cruiser's radio crackled. Chloe didn't understand the entire message, delivered in clipped jargon, but she caught the words *cat, tree* and *Sarah Culpepper.* When she turned to the deputy for explanation, he concentrated on his driving as if it were his first time behind the wheel. To Chloe's surprise, the tips of his ears were a deep shade of pink.

He cut her a glance. "I have a stop to make before I drop you off. You can stay in the car."

"Is it a dangerous situation?"

"No."

"What is it, then?"

He remained silent.

Chloe suspected he had an amazing capacity to stonewall. Well, she had an amazing capacity to persist. "You don't get to pick and choose what I see this week, Deputy. I'm here to record the good, the bad and the ugly." She reached in her backpack for her Nikon.

"Put that thing away and I'll explain."

She did as he ordered, telling herself he hadn't specified for how long.

"It all began," he said, clearly exasperated, "when Bonita Culpepper bought her granny a cell phone after a talk given at the seniors' center. On personal safety."

"Cell phones for the elderly. That sounds like a

good suggestion." She heard a click in her pocket. "Wait! Wait!" Quickly she removed the finished tape from the tiny recorder, then rummaged in her other pocket for a spare.

"Sarah Culpepper makes good use of her phone," he continued, ignoring her. He certainly didn't follow instructions very well. "No matter what her trouble is, she thinks she has a direct line to me."

"Who can you turn to if you can't turn to the sheriff?" she asked as she found a spare tape and jammed it in the recorder.

"Miss Sarah and I go back a long way. To when I was a boy. I'm not sure she sees me as a cop. As an adult, even. To her, I'm the neighbor's kid Mack, and I'm the one who always shinnied up her tree to rescue her cats."

"She had a cell phone when you were a boy?"

"No. She lives on a slip of property that abuts my family's homestead. She used to blow an old conch shell when she needed something."

"It's amazing that sound didn't scare the cats right out of the tree." Things were looking up. Chloe sat back in her seat and waited for events to unfold. She was about to see where Whittaker grew up and meet a woman who knew him as a boy. Now this might be a human-interest story in the making.

Mack sensed the smug satisfaction oozing from Chloe's side of the car, but there wasn't much he could do about it. Miss Sarah's house was coming up. He couldn't waste time or gas ferrying the reporter to town and driving back out here. For a cat. He pulled into the swept dirt front yard of the shotgun house. It sat in a grove of trees alongside the road to the Whittaker property.

He could hope the kid stayed in the cruiser. He could hope that, today, Miss Sarah's cat was easy to reach, giving the elderly woman less time to fill the reporter's head with tales of his youth. Hey, he could always hope he won the lottery while he was at it.

He pulled on the emergency brake. "This won't take long." His passenger had already cracked open her door. "You don't have to get out."

"All part of the story."

That was what he'd been afraid of.

"I hear meowing," she said.

"It'll be coming from the sweet-gum tree right over there. It usually is." He walked in the direction of the sound without checking to see if his shadow followed.

She did. "Is this the same cat you rescued as a boy?"

"Hardly." There'd been a succession of cats. All squirrel hunters. All with an uncanny inability to get down from a tree once they'd chased their prey up it. "All with the same name, though. Buster."

"Same tree?"

"Mostly." Mack looked toward the leafy canopy to discover not only Miss Sarah's cat stranded in the sweet gum, but Miss Sarah herself.

Her apron in a bunch around her middle, she clutched the tree trunk with one hand and her cell phone with the other. "You sure took your sweet time, Mack Whittaker."

He spotted the overturned kitchen chair at the base of the tree. "Now, why didn't you wait for me, Miss Sarah? Don't I always come?"

"Sooner or later." She hugged the tree trunk more tightly. "These days it's more often later than sooner."

"Deputy Whittaker had an emergency meeting at the high school," the kid piped up.

Miss Sarah squinted down from her precarious seat. "Who are you?"

"I'm Chloe Atherton, ma'am. From the *Western Carolina Sun*. I'm doing a story on the Colum County Sheriff's Department."

"Will I be in it?"

"Well, it sure looks as if you're part of the job." And right then and there, Kid Atherton had the nerve to take a picture of the old woman up a tree.

He grabbed the Nikon.

"Hey! Give that back!"

"Have a sense of decency," he muttered through clenched teeth.

"Give her back the camera, Mack," Miss Sarah ordered. "It's not often an old woman gets herself some attention."

When he handed it over, the reporter examined it carefully. "Ms. Culpepper," she said, with a none-too-happy glance in his direction, "this is a digital camera, so you can preview the photos. I'll erase any you're not happy with."

"Suits me fine," Miss Sarah retorted. Now *she* sent Mack a disapproving look.

He couldn't win.

"Ladies, if you'll excuse me." When he stepped under the low branch Miss Sarah sat on, his head reached her knees. "You can chat when both of you are on the ground." He held up his arms. "Push off, and I'll catch you."

Miss Sarah ignored him and concentrated, instead, on Chloe. "I'd like you to take a picture of Buster."

As if seconding that suggestion, a plaintive meow wafted from the upper branches.

Mack had endured enough of the niceties. "Ma'am, with all due respect, if you don't hop down—now—I'm going to leave and let the next big wind blow you and Buster out of this tree."

"You won't and you know it." Despite her assumption, she slid off the branch, anyway, and into his outstretched arms in a puff of nutmeg-scented flour. Flour and all, she must have weighed no more than ninety-five pounds.

"I declare," she said, dusting off her clothing with one hand and shaking her cell phone next to her ear with the other. "While you get Buster, Mack, let me see about hermit bars and sweet tea. Made 'em myself, you know."

"Thank you, but we won't be staying," he countered.

"Yes, you will." Miss Sarah beckoned to Chloe. "Girl, you can help me."

Reluctant to leave the two alone, he nonetheless swung himself up onto the lowest branch.

Once his footing was secure, he surveyed the surrounding landscape from his new perspective. Nothing adjusted your attitude faster than climbing a tree. Maybe that was why he didn't foist these cat-rescue missions off on one of the other deputies. For a few minutes every so often he got to feel like an innocent kid again in the branches of the Culpepper sweet gum.

He located Buster, hunkered down and suspicious, but within reach. Remembering the scratches this particular demon feline had inflicted last time, he cautiously wrapped his hands around the cat's middle. The Busters were the drawback to the tree-climbing respite.

HAVING TAKEN ONLY ONE mouthwatering bite of a homemade hermit, Chloe set the still-warm bar on a paper napkin to photograph Whittaker slowly maneuvering the branches with an indignant tabby in his arms. He'd left his hat in the car, and his dark, wind-ruffled hair no longer looked regulation. Although the climb in the tree had taken some of the starch and press out of his uniform, he still looked like a man used to commanding authority.

Sarah Culpepper stood beside Chloe on the narrow back porch and wiped her hands on her apron. "Despite the scrapes he's been in, that boy was destined to be a lawman."

"Scrapes? What—"

"Weren't you listening?" Sarah snapped. "I *said* Mack was destined to become a lawman."

For a fleeting instant Chloe thought the deputy might have engineered this particular PR stop. "Always?" If dirt were to be dug, she had a week to do it.

"Well, I'm not saying he *always* acted out what he knew to be right," Sarah said as she lined up three tall glasses on the porch railing, then filled them with tea. "And as a boy, he did have a devilish sense of humor that sometimes compromised his better nature."

Humor? He'd been pretty taciturn to this point. Chloe looked in the deputy's direction. In one fluid motion, he lowered himself to the ground, then deposited Buster at his feet. Cricking his tale, the cat stalked haughtily a few paces away, then sat and began to wash himself. Chloe continued taking photos as Whittaker brought the kitchen chair back to the stoop.

"Thanks for entertaining Ms. Atherton," he said. To Chloe he added, "Time to go."

Chloe slipped a couple hermit bars in her pocket in case he meant it.

"Sit down." Sarah thrust a glass of sweet tea at the

deputy. "And you," she ordered Chloe, "need to go get that picture of Buster. Make sure his eyes are open. He has beautiful gold eyes."

Chloe was quick to comply. When she'd taken several photos of the cat, she hurried back to show Sarah, only to find her deep in conversation with Whittaker, who was actually chuckling.

Seeing Chloe, he stopped short, then drained his glass. When he turned toward the cruiser, Sarah reached out to hold him back. "I was about to tell Chloe about your devilish sense of humor," she said.

"Don't believe a word of it." Mack ran his fingers through his close-cropped hair, resignation settling over his features.

"Well, Myron Hapes had a workshop behind his house," Sarah began. "A shed, really. Used to relax after a day of delivering the mail by doing woodwork in the evenings. Now when nature called, he'd avail himself of an old outhouse on the back of his property. If Estelle Hapes knew I was telling you this, she'd have a cow, especially seeing how proud she is of that new twenty-thousand-dollar bathroom she had put in off the master bedroom."

How was this shaggy-dog tale going to connect with Whittaker, and how was he going to react? Chloe wondered. Right now his arms were crossed and his eyes were closed as if he was writing up the report of the recent high-school meeting in his head.

"Come October," the elderly woman continued,

"Mack carves a jack-o'-lantern, lights it and puts it in Myron's outhouse after dark. Nearly gave the poor man a coronary. Mack was all of six. My, but I can tell you tales… So can most of the neighbors."

"I paid my debt to society," the deputy deadpanned. "Washed and waxed Mr. Hapes's Pontiac every Saturday for four weeks."

"Funny," Chloe said, getting into the spirit. "Perhaps I should follow up on this. Discover what other former scoundrels are now county leaders."

Whittaker froze. "Are you here to dig up dirt? Or are you here to write about a department in transition?"

"A good story's always worth the investigation."

Even Sarah bristled. "Well, you won't find any dirt on the sheriff or Mack. They are truly Colum County's finest. Why, Mack's a war hero. Got the medals to prove it."

"That and a dollar-fifty will get Ms. Atherton—"

"Chloe," she said.

"Chloe—" he repeated her first name as if it were strictly against regulations "—a cup of coffee at Rachel's Diner. We need to get you back to the B and B. Afternoon, Miss Sarah. Thanks for the tea." Abruptly he marched out to the patrol car.

When Chloe started to follow him, Ms. Culpepper asked, "You're not here to make trouble, are you?"

"No, ma'am. I plan to write the facts."

"There's facts and then there's truth."

"I'll keep that in mind."

She'd found the human-interest core to her story.

CHAPTER THREE

"DID YOU HURT YOURSELF climbing that tree?" Chloe asked.

Mack started. Damn, he'd blocked the extra presence out of the cruiser. "No. I didn't hurt myself." He pressed down on the accelerator.

He needed to check back at the office and have a quick briefing with the staff. A heads-up concerning this article, which was becoming more intrusive than he'd anticipated. He needed to see Tanya. And he needed to remember not to call this kid reporter *Chloe* as she'd insisted. More than the familiarity rattled him. The name itself was unsettling. Feminine and faintly seductive. When he'd said it, it had nearly pulled him out of business mode.

"Where do you live?"

Her simple question caught him off guard. "What does that have to do with your story?"

"Everything has to do with my story until I sort out my notes and choose a central theme."

"I thought we agreed the focus would be the department. The team."

"That's what you want it to be."

He'd seen how Atherton's face had lit up while Miss Sarah was talking. Reporters loved to chase human-interest stories the way Buster loved to chase squirrels. So let this rookie reporter humanize Breckinridge's story, or McMillan's or Sooner's. His was confidential. There were some things even the electorate had no right to know. He winced as he thought of Miss Sarah describing him as a war hero.

Atherton reached out and ran her fingers lightly over the instruments on the patrol car's dashboard, distracting him.

"Don't touch," he snapped.

"You or the dashboard?" she asked, pulling her hand back. "Where do you live?"

"Not in one of the expensive new developments," he replied, ticked at himself for explaining. "So you can stop suspecting misappropriation of department funds." Make that double-ticked for elaborating.

"Where, then?" She rolled her window down. Then up. Then halfway down. Then settled in to review the photos she'd taken. "The question's not out of line. A big issue in many metro areas is that teachers, firefighters and police officers often can't afford to live in the neighborhoods they service. Is it the same in Colum County?"

"Above the office there's a small barracks. I live there."

She plunked the Nikon in her lap. "Do the other deputies?" The surprise in her voice warned him to be cautious.

"Not full-time," he admitted.

"Why do you?"

"Because I'm married to my job." He wasn't about to tell her how the sheriff, afraid Mack might backslide into alcohol, had installed him in the barracks. When his life had stabilized, Mack hadn't seen much point in moving, although his parents kept bugging him about how they kept his room at the farmhouse available, should he ever want to return home.

Thankfully, the bed-and-breakfast came into view. He pulled the cruiser to a head-snapping halt in front.

"Deputy Whittaker?"

Without enthusiasm, he turned to look at his passenger. He could use a drink.

"Your doubts about our working together wouldn't come from the fact that I'm a woman, would it?" she asked.

He gritted his teeth. Working with women—either in the department or in the army—had never been a problem. But how could he say so now without sounding defensive? "I'm sure we'll get along fine."

"Good. See you tomorrow." She got out of the car, but left her scent behind. Light. Appealing. Like fresh-baked goods. Simpler days.

He didn't answer her. Didn't set a time for their meeting again. Didn't look in her direction. As soon as he heard her door click, he put the patrol car in gear. Automatic drive.

Chloe watched as Deputy Whittaker drove away, not like a cop, but like a hotrodder. The man was as thorny and closed as a pinecone after the rain. Why, back at Ms. Culpepper's, when Chloe had suggested he call her by her first name, had he not made the slightest, begrudging suggestion she call him Mack? And why had he gone all wooden when the elderly woman mentioned his combat medals? Unless the other deputies proved as intriguing, Chloe was determined to follow Whittaker until she had him—and the pull he exerted in the county—figured out.

Shouldering her heavy backpack, she made her way up the front walk to the bed-and-breakfast, a rambling two-story structure that, despite the rockers on the front porch and the planters still filled with winter pansies, looked as if it might once have been a saloon. Chloe wasn't sure whether June Parker would be offended or amused by that observation.

Chloe was fascinated by the owner. Part nineteenth-century sweet magnolia and part savvy twenty-first-century businesswoman, Ms. Parker was an exquisitely groomed woman of indeterminate age. As well as running a bed-and-breakfast, she apparently gave comportment lessons to the town children and headed an investment club for retired women—discreet signs at the front desk advertised as much.

"Afternoon, Miss Atherton." Wearing a large sun hat, hot-pink Crocs, gardening gloves and an apron that read "I'm not old—I just need repotting," Ms. Parker knelt in a flower bed. "Will you join us for tea at four? Everything on my tea cart is homemade."

Chloe shouldn't have eaten so many of Sarah Culpepper's hermit bars. "Of course," she replied, unwilling to miss an opportunity to gather information. "Do I have time to freshen up?"

Ms. Parker checked a delicate antique watch pinned to her blouse. "We both do. I'll see you in the parlor in thirty minutes."

Chloe retreated to her room, grateful for the small luxuries her hostess had provided. Hand-milled soaps, fluffy towels for a quick wash and a big, sensuously soft bed scented with crabapple blossoms from the gardens below. The April breezes ruffled the sheer curtains by the open window and acted as a narcotic, quickly lulling her into a deep, dreamless sleep when she'd only intended a catnap.

She awoke abruptly, wondering if it might be morning—and time to meet up with that puzzling deputy—until she smelled the pungent bergamot aroma of Earl Grey, mingled with baking spices. She found herself unexpectedly ravenous. Both for food and for information. Hopping out of bed and glancing in the mirror, she ran her fingers through her hair, then dashed downstairs to find Ms. Parker presiding at a silver tea set. Although a three-tiered sandwich and pastry tray held enough food for, if not an army, then a battalion, the innkeeper was the only person in the room.

"I'm sorry. I overslept," Chloe explained. "Did I miss everyone?"

"Not at all," Ms. Parker replied, pouring hot tea into a translucent china cup. "We're only two today. Mondays aren't particularly busy."

Chloe accepted the tea and a seat on a chair covered in petit point at a table set with linen and fresh flowers. "And you went to all this trouble."

"Trouble? I hardly think a civilized break in the middle of the day can be categorized as *trouble.* If I had no guests at all, I'd do this for myself. Call it part of my mental health program."

No wonder you couldn't tell June Parker's age. She knew how to take care of herself. If Chloe hadn't moved on to harder news, June would have made a lovely subject for the paper's Living section.

"But all these goodies…" Chloe indicated the extravagant tea tray.

"At the end of the day I send what's left over to the sheriff's office. Those hardworking deputies deserve some TLC."

An opening.

"About Mack Whittaker…"

"Him especially."

Chloe was taken aback. If ever there was an individual who appeared able to look after himself, who appeared not to need—or notice—the softer things in life, that was Deputy Whittaker.

"Mack recently served in Iraq," Ms. Parker explained.

"Ah, yes. Ms. Culpepper said he'd received medals." Chloe nibbled on a cranberry-orange scone. Heaven. "Can you tell me what they were for?"

"I could. But you should have Mack tell you." The inn owner fingered the delicate lace edging on her linen napkin. "Applegate is one big family, Ms. Atherton. Of course we talk among ourselves. But unless we know your daddy, granddaddy and great-granddaddy, we're not going to talk to you behind a family member's back."

Chloe's opened her eyes wide. Well. Now she knew where she stood. Whittaker's medals she could research. But it intrigued her that this was the third time today she'd met apparent admiration for the deputy, tempered with a reluctance to talk about him.

"Perhaps we could switch to first names," Ms. Parker said, "and you could tell me about yourself."

Chloe fidgeted in her seat. Without her backpack and her tools of the trade, she felt exposed. She had made herself strong by becoming an observer and never liked being the object of attention.

"Were you born and raised around here?" June persisted.

"No. I'm from Atlanta originally. My father's a mathematics professor at Emory and my mother's an epidemiologist at the CDC—Centers for Disease Control. I'm a reporter, and that's about all there is to tell," she finished in one long breath.

June smiled over the rim of her teacup. "I'm sure there's more to the story than that."

"We're a family that sticks to the facts," Chloe replied with a twinge of discomfort. "To that end…I'm in town to learn about the sheriff's department. Its procedures. Its personnel."

"I certainly hope you're not planning to rummage around in Mack's personal pain to sell papers," the innkeeper said, putting her teacup down with a sharp snick.

Chloe didn't back down. "I'm searching for the right angle. Whether it's the town itself, the sheriff's department or the individuals who make up that department."

"Then you'd better head to the town meeting tonight. There'll be enough topics there for several articles."

Chloe cocked her head. Why hadn't the deputy mentioned the town meeting? For his lack of disclosure alone, she wouldn't miss it.

FROM WHERE HE STOOD IN the corner at the back of the hall, Mack noticed Atherton, dragging her battered backpack, squeeze through the entranceway.

How did she get wind of the meeting?

Unsuccessfully, she looked around for a seat, then began to mingle with the crowd that always formed at the back of the room. The folks who came to shoot the breeze as if there wasn't an official meeting going on in the front. Mack took a count of those citizens nearest the reporter who might be counted gossips. Three notorious talkers. Damn.

Making space for latecomers, Myron Hapes stepped closer to Mack. "I hear," the retired postal worker said, leaning in, "Frank Hudson's getting up a petition to turn the county dry. What do you think his chances are?"

"Slim to none." Mack let out a groan as he saw Atherton moving in his direction.

"I know you probably would rather liquor weren't so readily available," Mryon said, not bothering to lower his voice. "A dry county would make your job easier. Maybe would have made it less easy for you to turn to the stuff."

Tearing his attention from the approaching reporter, Mack glowered at Myron.

"Sorry, Mack. I didn't mean to dredge up ancient history."

So why did people always do it? And now, especially, with the fourth estate on the prowl.

"I gotta talk to Frank," Myron said hastily, then retreated into the crowd.

Only to be replaced by Atherton. "Nice of you to

mention there was a meeting tonight," she said, her words laced with accusation.

"It slipped my mind." He pretended to concentrate on Deputy Darden, who was at the front of the room answering a question on speed bumps.

"I wanted to ask you—"

"Shh!"

"Don't shush me! I'm not a child."

"There's a meeting going on, in case you hadn't noticed."

She scanned the groups milling by the door, then rolled her eyes. "As if I didn't know the real stuff gets done in these back-of-the-room cabals."

He'd have to look that word up in the sheriff's crossword dictionary.

He looked at his watch. Tanya was expecting him. "I'll answer your questions tomorrow," he said. "Right now I'm off duty." He could only hope she understood he was entitled to a private life.

But the expression in her eyes was one of disbelief. "When you said you were married to the job—"

"Even married folks need an occasional break." He inspected her upturned face, suspecting she might be someone else as dedicated to her job as he was. It was his bad luck she regarded *him* as her job. Without engaging in further chat, he made his way out of the room.

So what did a workaholic public servant do off duty?

Was that even pertinent to her article? Shouldn't she stay here and soak in some of the town flavor? Suss out the issues? Meet the residents who were directly affected by the local law?

At the front of the room—in the official meeting—people were hotly debating methods for slowing traffic on the main drag. Yawn. The back of the room wasn't much better. Talk of feed prices, boundary disputes, the sheriff's wedding and some investment scheme making the rounds. Double yawn.

She gave him a couple of minutes' head start, then slipped out of the room. At the entrance to the town hall, she observed him making his way across the parking lot to his cruiser. Not a private vehicle. And the deputy was off duty. Was that by the book? She'd have to check. Something else came to mind. She hadn't caught all of Whittaker's conversation when she'd come upon him in the meeting hall, but she thought she'd heard the man he'd been talking to mention something about Whittaker's having turned to liquor. A joke, or serious? If it had been serious, what did it have to do with the execution of the man's duties?

If he was on the up-and-up, he had nothing to hide from her investigation.

As she made her way to the Yugo, she felt a twinge of doubt. Was this investigative reporting…or was this creative nonfiction? Had she singled out Whittaker because he was the deputy in charge or because he was an enigma? That fact-finding challenge she so loved. A man the residents of Applegate relied on, respected and worried about. A man who softened—slightly—only when he was up a tree, rescuing a tomcat.

June Parker had warned her not to use Whittaker's pain to sell papers. But the woman couldn't have known the personal pain that drove Chloe to uncover the facts and dispel speculation.

As the deputy pulled out of the parking lot, she put her own car in gear. Firsthand observation led to facts. The facts, once they fell into a pattern, would constitute the truth. And the truth, however painful, was the foundation of life.

Following at a discreet distance, she was mildly surprised when he didn't pull into the sheriff's office parking lot but continued through town. On the outskirts, where the streetlights ended, he turned left and crossed the railroad tracks. A full planter's moon provided the only real light.

Chloe knew that in many small towns in the south, "the wrong side of the tracks" wasn't merely an expression. Despite its new upscale subdivisions, Applegate still had a seamier side, and this was it. Not part of the groomed in-town neighborhoods, but not rural farmland, either. The road meandered between houses too close together and in need of repair.

The evening being mild for April, Chloe rolled her

window down. Many of the residents clustered on front stoops—talking, drinking, smoking or listening to music. Although it was fairly late and a school night, kids were everywhere. Adolescent boys with attitude hung with men who eyed the women. The women eyed them right back. The aromas of barbecue and simmering salsa melded with a sweet scent Chloe knew couldn't be legal. Didn't Deputy Whittaker smell it? If so, he didn't stop.

About a mile down the road, as the houses became less regularly spaced, the cruiser slowed, then came to a stop in front of one particular house, its weedy front yard strewn with plastic toys. The deputy got out of his patrol car and walked over to a woman leaning on the front porch railing. Her hair was big…her tank top small. And her jeans looked as if they'd been painted on. In the porch light she looked tired.

Chloe slowed the Yugo as she drove past.

Mack Whittaker pulled his wallet out of his back pocket, took out several bills and handed them to the woman. Stuffing the money in her top, she slid her arm around his back and drew him into the house.

Now what was Chloe to make of that firsthand observation?

CHAPTER FOUR

THE DAY WAS ALREADY HOT as hell. The terrain outside the military tent was dry, sand-choked and godforsaken. Several of the guys in his unit were engaged in a game of poker before heading out on patrol. Mack couldn't understand the attraction to games of chance. Not here. When every breath you took was a gamble. But who was he to judge? Nate, looking up from his hand, had razzed him for opting for a shower—if you could call it that, what with the rationed water. What's the point, Nate had asked, when you're gritty again two seconds later? Maybe Mack persevered because, for a few moments, he could close his eyes and imagine himself back in Applegate.

The explosion rocked the encampment as he was peeling off his T-shirt. Bare-chested, he ran out of the shower area. Plumes of black smoke rose to embrace the relentless Iraqi sun. Rose from the spot where his tent had been. Where the guys had been playing poker minutes ago…

With a howl to wake the dead, Mack sat bolt

upright. In the dark and drenched in sweat, he couldn't tell what was real or what was dream until a door opened and Deputy McMillan stuck his head in. The shaft of light illuminated the wall of lockers, the cots—all empty except for the one Mack clung to, in the barracks room he'd called home for the past six months.

"Whittaker, you okay?"

Mack was shaking so hard he was afraid he might bite off his tongue if he tried to answer.

"The morning shift's about to come in," McMillan drawled, feigning nonchalance, Mack knew. "I'm makin' coffee. Take a shower. You can get a hit of caffeine when you're done." The deputy disappeared, leaving the overhead light off, but the door ajar.

Mack put both feet on the floor. He hated that the other deputies tiptoed around him. Hated that they appeared to be waiting patiently for an explanation. Of his continued squatting in the barracks. Of his silence about his tour of duty. Of his night terrors.

His head now throbbing, he stripped and stepped into the shower. Let the harsh stream of cold water sluice over his body, numbing him. When he returned to his cot, a mug of fresh coffee sat on the nightstand. A small act of compassion that compounded his guilt.

He gulped the coffee as he dressed, then headed downstairs to the sheriff's office. He'd pick up something to eat on the go because he didn't want to hang around the kitchen for breakfast as the shifts changed and the deputies congregated with stories about family or nights carousing or days off fishing. He might be fit for duty, but he wasn't up to faking the rest.

As he approached Kim Nash, engaged in animated conversation with... Damn, he'd forgotten all about the kid.

Dressed in penny loafers—he didn't know they still made them—trousers made of some silky khaki material and a long-sleeved white shirt with a flowing scarf tied at her neck, Chloe Atherton didn't look as if she belonged in the twenty-first century. She looked like an actress right out of the 1940s. One of those earnest ingenues trying hard to make it in a man's world. The one who always cracked the hard-boiled hero's shell. God, he'd spent too many sleepless nights watching old black-and-white movies on the barracks TV.

"Good morning, Deputy!" Atherton sang out as she pocketed her notepad. "I'm ready when you are."

He wasn't ready. Not for her. Or her constant questions. Not again.

"Come on," he said, thinking on his feet. "You're going to want to meet Breckinridge. For a female perspective on the force. You can shadow her today."

There was no mistaking the glint of interest in the reporter's eyes. Good. Breckinridge's life was such a colorful and open book, she often talked about writing her memoirs. Maybe when she was older and had begun to slow down. This interview would give her fifteen minutes of fame *now*. Moreover, it would eat up one more day of Atherton's stay, and it would keep her prying eyes away from him.

"I have a couple questions about The Program," she said, trying to keep pace with him.

"Breckinridge can answer them," he replied, moving toward the windowless room where his coworker sat behind a mountain of paperwork. "You'll find the deputies interchangeable. Breckinridge, meet Atherton," Mack said. "From the *Western Carolina Sun*. The sheriff's given her open access to the department this week. Today's your day to show her the ropes."

Breckinridge threw up her hands in mock surprise. "So you *do* have a heart, Whittaker. I was beginning to worry how I was going to survive my shift, stuck in this hole alone. I hate filing."

"We all do," he replied, turning to leave. "That's why we rotate." He felt the reporter's hand on his arm.

"I don't think this interview will take all day."

"You never know," he replied, shaking her off. "These are incident reports. Every one tells a story. There's no one better at fleshing out a story than Breckinridge. After today, you'll have a real feel for our work."

Breckinridge eyed him suspiciously, but said nothing.

Avoiding looking at Atherton, Mack got out of the room while the getting was good.

Chloe tried to open her backpack to retrieve her tape recorder, but she pulled the zipper so hard it jammed. "I think he was trying to get rid of me."

"Don't take it personally," Deputy Breckinridge replied, grabbing a handful of file folders. "Whittaker's basically a loner."

"How can that be? One of the first things he said to me was how the department constituted a team. He emphasized that."

"At work he is a team player. Absolutely. But…PR isn't his strength. Sheriff McQuire usually handles all that."

"Then why would Sheriff McQuire put Deputy Whittaker in charge when he knew I'd be here on assignment for the week?"

"The sheriff and Whittaker were friends long before they worked together. If you ask me, the assignment is kind of a personal rehabilitation—" Breckinridge stopped abruptly. "That's off the record."

Why would Mack need rehab?

"If you'd rough sort these by case number—" Breckinridge, any confidential attitude gone, indicated the folders covering the small desk "—I'll file them and give you an indication of the types of situations we handle."

Because the deputy balked at discussing Mack further, Chloe agreed to help, then spent the morning alternately filing and filling her tape recorder and notebook with details of movement of prisoners at the county jail, assistance in court proceedings, domestic disputes, traffic accidents and the ongoing county fight against illegal substances. Although Breckinridge—she'd eventually insisted Chloe call her Hannah—was a font of department information, besides being very forthcoming about her own colorful off-duty life, Chloe felt dissatisfied. The police stuff was good background, but it wasn't a story. And although Hannah's life was a plot and a half, it didn't particularly affect the dynamics of Colum County law enforcement.

On the other hand, Deputy Whittaker's relationship with Sheriff McQuire might merit a feature article. Cronyism, perhaps? Was the sheriff carrying his friend for some reason?

"I can't believe we finished this job," Hannah declared several hours later. "I appreciate the assist. You want to break for lunch upstairs? Tacos. Darden's specialty."

"No, thanks." Chloe looked at her ink-smeared fingertips. "I'd like to wash up, then interview some of the business owners along Main Street. Get a feel for their concerns."

"Suit yourself. If you have any more questions, I'm here on desk duty for the rest of my shift."

"I do have one more question. You said Deputy Whittaker was a loner off the job. Has that always been the case?"

Hannah's expression became guarded, and she

made a show of straightening the miscellaneous items remaining on the desk.

"I mean, you love people." Chloe hastened to reframe her question. "It's obvious from talking with you this morning. You feel a connection to the citizens of Applegate. So I'd like to know how a loner like Whittaker chooses a career in public service."

"Mack wasn't always a loner." Doodling on the blotter, the deputy examined her cartoon and chose her words carefully. "I was a couple years behind him in high school. He was the big man on campus. Sports star. The guy all the girls fell for. It didn't hurt he had a killer smile on top of that ripped body. He loved practical jokes, fast cars and parties. He loved life." She looked up at Chloe and shrugged. "It was fun being around him."

The kind of guy who'd made Chloe's high-school days uncomfortable at best.

Shy as a girl, she'd had no social skills as an underclassman in high school. When she discovered the school newspaper in her junior year, she didn't suddenly blossom, she found protection in the power of the pen. Her writing gave her leverage, discipline and detachment to cope with her family's shared pain and her own adolescent angst. And the where-withal to eventually grow strong.

"So what happened?" Chloe asked, now curious about why a former social creature had gone cold and distant. "To Whittaker."

"I don't know. Although…I think it must have had to do with his tour of duty in Iraq. But I don't think even Sheriff McQuire knows." Hannah slapped her hands on the desk and stood. "Hey, I'm starving. Sure I can't interest you in a couple tacos?"

"No, thanks." Chloe loaded up her backpack and accompanied Hannah as far as the stairs.

Determined to be the one to get the answer to the deputy's turnaround, Chloe found it ironic that with this article on the sheriff's department, she—the former insecure nerd—now had potential power over a man such as Mack Whittaker.

As THE CLOCK ON THE county courthouse struck four, Mack lowered himself onto a stool at the far end of the counter in Rachel's Diner. When he caught Rachel's eye, he nodded toward the coffeepot. Although mid-afternoon customers chatted amiably across the room as if they weren't at separate tables, no one spoke to him. Oh, they'd all recognized him with a nod or a wave as he'd entered, but unless he initiated conversation, they knew to leave him alone—a reflex from his six months as a belligerent drunk.

"Cheer up," Rachel said, setting a mug of steaming coffee in front of him. "Only five more days in the public eye." Rachel was one of very few people in town who didn't pay any attention to the wall he'd put up. The sheriff's new wife, Samantha, was another.

"And you have it lucky," the owner of the diner continued. "You know the end will come. Sam didn't know if those vultures would ever leave her alone."

Yeah, the paparazzi certainly had descended on Applegate when they'd discovered Samantha was a hotel empire heiress. The poor woman had come to Applegate under an assumed name to turn her life around. Not only had she turned her life around, and Garrett's, she'd dragged Mack to AA and a reckoning of his own.

He kept his head down and took a long, slow sip of coffee.

Rachel didn't accept the brush-off. "There's only one in this new wave, sure," she said, standing right across the counter from him and vigorously polishing the salt and pepper shakers with a paper towel, as if she had nothing else to do. No other customers to harass. "I guess you could consider her marginally local. But she's as tenacious as that whole pack of national newshounds. Look at her out there."

Mack followed Rachel's gaze out the front plate-glass window to the bench next to the laundromat across the street, where Atherton sat, writing in a notebook. There were a dozen benches along Main Street. So why did the woman choose this particular one? And how had she escaped Breckinridge?

"She was in here earlier," Rachel said. "Asking about you."

"About me?" He turned his back to the window

and tried to tamp down his rising displeasure. "Damned article's supposed to be about the department," he muttered. Maybe if he ignored the source of his irritation, she'd go away.

"The conversation was odd from the beginning," Rachel mused, pouring herself a cup of coffee, then leaning on the counter. Mack resigned himself to a long story. It was better than the alternative— walking out of the diner and having his shadow reattach.

"Her questions were roundabout at first," Rachel continued. "A setup. Because what she wanted was information on you."

"How so?"

"Well, first she asked about Burt."

"Burt?" Burt Jones was a Vietnam vet who lived alone up in Beecham's Hollow. On his meds, he was an accomplished handyman. Off, he wandered aimlessly. Earlier this afternoon he'd been in town, medicated and purposeful. "What could she possibly want to know about him?"

"As I said, I couldn't figure her real motives. Especially when she switched the subject to Duke Donahue."

Damn. Duke was Tanya's oldest. The teenager had been hit hard by his father's death and had been in and out of trouble recently. Shoplifting. Vandalism. Recreational drugs. Two suspensions from school. But he was beginning to show signs of coming out of this self-destructive behavior. He didn't need any aspect of his story splashed across the pages of the *Sun*.

Mack dug into his pocket to pay for his coffee. It was time he straightened out Ms. Chloe Atherton.

"It's on the house." Rachel pushed his money back across the counter. "There's more."

Puzzled, he looked at her. He'd almost forgotten he wasn't alone. "What did you tell the reporter about Burt and Duke?"

"Nothing." Rachel turned one shoulder to him as if offended. "She'd already gotten their names from someone else. But as I said, you were her angle. I understood she'd seen you with both Burt and Duke."

"I talked to them at different times this afternoon, yeah. In broad daylight. On Main Street. So what's the big deal?"

"She wanted to know if there *was* a big deal. Why you'd be taking money from Burt. Why you'd be giving money to Duke."

The Atherton woman had gone too far. In that instant he stopped thinking of her as an innocent kid.

Leaving his money on the counter, he turned to go, only to discover the bench in front of the laundromat was empty.

She wasn't getting off that easily.

He stepped next door to headquarters. Not there.

Back on Main Street, he marched the couple of blocks to June's bed-and-breakfast. For the life of him, he couldn't figure out what the reporter was up to. Could it be she was no more ethical than the paparazzi who'd harried Samantha?

Inside the inn, he stopped short at the sight of Ms. Parker presiding over tea in her front parlor with several guests. Atherton wasn't among them.

"She's in the back garden," the owner said quietly, a definite look of interest—collusion?—on her face.

If Chloe Atherton thought she could hide behind June Parker's skirts, she had another think coming.

Mack stormed through the familiar old house, into the kitchen and out the back door. From the stoop he could see Atherton sitting on the swing under the big oak tree in the very back of the garden. Her arms wrapped around the swing's thick ropes, she was listening to a tape recorder in one hand while jotting notes with the other.

He saw red.

"What the hell do you think you're doing?" he demanded, striding toward her, his boots scattering pebbles on the well-groomed path.

"The very question I wanted to ask you," she replied, hopping off the swing to face him.

"Me? I'm not the one prying into everyone's personal business."

Standing practically toe-to-toe with him, she didn't bat an eyelash. "I haven't determined yet what's personal and what's of public interest."

"So you'll cast a wide net regardless of who might

get hurt? Burt. Duke. What have they got to do with your story on the department?"

"You tell me." Her gray eyes were filled with shadows. "Why would a sheriff's deputy accept cash, a rather sizable chunk, from a man some describe as a vagrant, then turn around and give cash to a kid who's been suspended from school for drugs?"

So she had been tailing him. And talking to more people than Rachel. He didn't know whether to throttle the reporter or the local gossips when he found out who they were.

"That wasn't a rhetorical question," she insisted as he eyed her in stony silence.

He clenched his hands at his sides so that he didn't reach out for her notebook and recorder. Didn't throw them on the ground and grind them under his boot heel. "From one afternoon's observation, you think I'm both on the take and buying drugs."

"I don't know. I saw something that could or could not be deemed suspicious. I'd like to hear your explanation. Especially, since you claimed when I first met you, that this new department was squeaky clean. And for this week, at least, you're the face of the department."

Clearly the woman had her sights set on a career beyond the *Sun*. On a tabloid career. "Both Burt and Duke have had a rough go of it. Leave them out of your story."

"And the cash?"

She wasn't going to give up until she had her answer, and he wasn't going to let her threaten either Burt's or Duke's tenuous hold on rehabilitation. Better she learn something personal about him.

"Burt was repaying a loan I made him to see him through between jobs. And Duke…I rewarded him for a decent report card." Finally.

"Relatives of yours?"

"Friends," he replied through gritted teeth.

"Do you see how easily you cleared up this misconception?" she asked, tilting her head so that her strawberry-blond hair swung gracefully to one side. She spoke with a faint smile as if the two of them were friends, too. Who moved easily from a minor disagreement back to compatibility.

What he felt was poles apart from friendship. "Why didn't you ask me before jumping to conclusions?"

"That's the sad part." She sighed dramatically and played with the ends of the blue silk scarf tied around her neck. "You made it perfectly clear you didn't want me around."

"I did not."

"Then why did you foist me off on Deputy Breckinridge?"

"To get a woman's perspective on the department."

She regarded him as if she didn't believe it.

Mack inhaled sharply as an ugly thought began to dawn. "You were snooping around, deliberately creating drama this afternoon—which you knew would get back to me eventually—because you were ticked that I wasn't giving you my full attention. Maybe you thought you could find something you could use as—I hesitate to use the word *blackmail*—leverage?"

She stuck her finger in the center of his chest. And pushed. "I'm not that kind of reporter. I was simply doing my job as best I could—alone—once it became evident you weren't taking my assignment seriously. An assignment, I might remind you, your boss requested."

When it looked as if she might poke him again, he took a step backward. "Lady, don't try to throw your weight around. I'm bigger than you by a good hundred pounds."

Her cheeks flamed red, making the freckles across her nose stand out. "I'm not going away, Deputy Whittaker. I'm staying right here in town for the next five days. My article about your department—and that includes you—and its relationships with the citizens of this town *will* appear in the paper. With or without your help."

He thought of Duke and Burt and how easily Atherton's journalistic point might lead to real hurt. He thought of Samantha and how the press had nearly ruined her new life in Applegate. He thought of his own recent past.

"Real reporting is one thing," he said. "Tabloid bottom-feeding is another. How would you like someone digging into your background? Not necessarily looking for substance or the truth, but just scratching the surface until something titillating turned up?"

Her notebook slipped out of her hand and clattered to the stone path. Before she bent to retrieve it, he thought he saw a flicker of…doubt? Pain? Fear?

"Tomorrow morning," she said, rising, once again composed, "I'll be at headquarters. Seven sharp as the shifts change. You can tell me then if I can expect your cooperation."

She didn't look at him as she gathered her things and stowed them in her backpack. "Now I'm going inside to organize my notes. And to give you time to come to your senses."

With the bearing of a person twice her stature, she swept by him and into the house.

Leaving him stunned at the dismissal.

"Let me come to my senses?" he shouted after her when he finally found his voice. "Let me come to my—"

He stopped bellowing when June Parker's face popped up at the kitchen window.

"I—I'm sorry, Ms. Parker," he said.

"Don't be," she said brightly. "It's good to see you're back from the dead."

CHAPTER FIVE

OMINOUS CLOUDS HUNG OVERHEAD as Chloe, cell phone pressed to her ear, hastened down Main Street past stores that wouldn't open for several hours yet. The early morning call from her editor, Deirdre Kinkaid, was going on much longer than Chloe thought necessary. If this made her late for the change in shifts at the sheriff's department…

Trouble was, she'd mentioned to Deirdre how the deputy was resisting her attempts to find the story's center, and Deirdre had immediately begun to rethink her decision to move Chloe from the Living section to special reports.

"You have to be tougher, Chloe," Deirdre insisted. "As a woman—and a petite woman, at that—you have to work extra hard to project the *gravitas* that will gain you respect…"

Blah, blah, blah. Chloe had heard all this before. Her name was too soft, her stature too unimposing, her face too girlish to be taken seriously. Well, it wasn't true, and this article was the opportunity to prove the lie.

And with Mack's uncomfortable counter-questioning yesterday into how she'd feel if someone rummaged around in her past, she was determined to remain steadfastly professional. She was proud that the *Sun* had never had to print a retraction for one of her articles. She, of all people, knew the hurt that ill-researched reporting could cause.

"I'm sorry, Deirdre," she said, interrupting her editor's monologue at the front door of the sheriff's department, "but the reception is awful in this valley. You're breaking up. I'll e-mail an update. Bye."

Once inside the building, she was confronted with a hubbub of activity. Staff from both the morning and the graveyard shifts came and went with serious glances at a large television on a wall in the central area, tuned to a weather channel. The map of the Southern U.S. now on the screen was overlaid with a pattern of yellow and red boxes. Chloe knew them well. Tornado watches and warnings.

Tough as she wanted to appear, she had a Southerner's deep-rooted apprehension of such forecasts.

Repositioning her backpack over one shoulder, she followed several deputies who were making their way to a meeting room on the far side. There she could see Mack making changes on a dry-erase board.

"Listen up!" he barked as the deputy behind Chloe closed the meeting-room door. "Some assignments have shifted. McMillan, you're still on desk. We have a pile of tips related to that fake-lottery-ticket scheme. I want you to begin making some sense of them. Sooner, you're still on patrol. West sector of the county. The story today is the approaching storm system. With the tornado watch in effect, we have to make sure the trailer park's on alert and any elderly folks living alone have a place to go if the watch is upgraded. Mind the skies, everyone."

Hands clasped behind his back, Mack began to pace at a podium bearing a large sheriff's department seal, his expression as dark as the lowering sky outside.

"Breckinridge, you and I are changing places," he said slowly as if this wasn't a decision he'd come to lightly. "You'll supervise transfer of prisoners at the courthouse, while I take the east sector patrol." He took a deep breath. "Ms. Atherton will be riding with me."

So, he'd come to his senses.

"The rest is as written on the board," he concluded. "The other shifts are on call if we need them. Stay alert."

Once the deputies began leaving, Chloe asked, "Why did you switch assignments with Breckinridge?"

"There's a lot that can go wrong when you're transferring prisoners," he replied, his demeanor hard and unyielding, in stark contrast to the passion he displayed the day before.

"And you didn't want me in the way," she finished for him.

"Transfer of prisoners is a dangerous business." He picked up his Stetson from the podium. "If you want to see that, you can review the surveillance videotapes."

He wasn't protecting her. It was obvious he was protecting the workings of his department. At the same time he'd given himself an assignment that would give her full access to him. She suspected that he hoped to direct the activities while keeping an eye on her. She was essentially being babysat.

Not a satisfying thought, especially after her conversation with Deirdre.

"Are you coming or not?" Standing in the meeting-room doorway, the deputy eyed her without a trace of emotion. How could someone that handsome be that cold?

Mack resented the energy it took to keep himself under control. Energy that would be better spent on his job. With a nasty storm system approaching, he needed to be a hundred places at once today, not reined in and distracted. But after his outburst yesterday, he absolutely knew he needed to keep his true feelings in check if the *Sun* article was to end up an honest depiction and not purple prose. Or personal profile.

"I'm coming," Atherton said, pulling the camera from her backpack. "What's first on our agenda?"

"You heard me in the briefing."

"We're patrolling the eastern part of the county," she said, pointing the expensive camera at him.

He turned his head, pretending to check the time

on the wall clock. "Leave me out of your photo shoots. By the end of the day, you'll have more-dramatic subjects than me."

"I'm checking my batteries," she replied, ignoring him. "Did you, by any chance, talk to the sheriff last night?"

"What do you mean?"

"I'm riding with you again. I thought he might have…encouraged it."

"I didn't talk to him." He didn't need Garrett ordering him to cooperate with this reporter. All on his own, he'd come to the painful decision to make himself "accessible." Impatiently he swept his hand toward the doorway.

"Do you think there's a real possibility of torna-does?" she asked as they made their way through the building and out to the parking lot. There was a nervous edge to her voice, leading him to believe she might not be as tough as she let on.

"It's a helluva system," he said. "And the barom-eter's already plunging."

"Will we be checking on Ms. Culpepper?" she asked, standing by the passenger's side of the patrol car, gazing at him across the roof, waiting for him to unlock her door.

"Yes, we'll be checking on her. And…" His parents. Great. Why did he have to assign himself the eastern sector? "Whistling Meadows."

"What's Whistling Meadows?"

Instead of unlocking the cruiser for her, he picked at a splatter of mud on the fender. If he was going to have to answer her questions, he might as well be forthcoming on the innocuous ones. "It's a llama farm. It belongs to the sheriff's wife."

"I know the runaway-heiress story."

So it wasn't an innocuous question. "She's nothing like y'all made her out," he snapped, unlocking the car and getting in. "You aren't going to resurrect that disaster, are you?"

"Puh-leeze!" she said, sliding into the seat beside him. She was becoming quite the annoying fixture in his daily routine. "Give me more credit than that."

Unsure whether she might harbor a reporter's curiosity for a behind-the-scenes tour, he considered skipping the check on Whistling Meadows. But Rory was stateside again and attending eighth grade under the McQuire housekeeper's care, while the man who used to own the farm was looking after the llamas until Garrett and Samantha got back from their honeymoon. Both Geneva and Red were getting on in years, and Mack would feel better if he saw for himself the three were all right.

In awkward silence, he and the reporter drove the few miles out of town to the llama farm.

A gust of wind hit the patrol car as Mack turned into the dirt drive that led to his friends' place. He could see Red helping Geneva take down laundry that flapped wildly on the lines beyond the kitchen stoop. The six llamas, normally curious and social where humans were concerned, were huddled together under a tree halfway up the slope of the inner pasture. They didn't pay the slightest attention to the cruiser. Animals had an eerie sixth sense about approaching bad weather.

He pulled to a stop in the farmyard as Geneva hurried into the house with a basket of laundry. Red came over to the driver's side of the car, and Mack rolled down the window. The air, loaded with moisture, smelled of humus. "Y'all okay up here?" Mack asked.

"We're fine," Red replied, eyeing Chloe with curiosity. "Got the weather channel on. Got the crank NOAA radio in case the power goes out. Got the root cellar if all hell breaks loose. But Geneva's worried about Rory. The bus picked up the kids as usual this morning. You think the school's gonna send 'em home early?"

"Call the board of ed."

Red stuck his arm across Mack's chest. "I'm Red Harris," he said to Chloe. "Farm manager."

"Pleased to meet you. I'm Chloe Atherton," she replied, shaking his hand. "From the *Western Carolina Sun.*"

"Ah." Red shot a sly smile at Mack. "The interview the sheriff dumped on our deputy here. Put him back in a foul mood with that announcement, I'll tell you. Two steps forward, one back. Glad to see he's rising to the occasion, though. Can't hurt that you're pretty."

"We have to shove off." His foot on the brake, Mack put the cruiser in gear. "As long as you're prepared."

"We are." Red had the brass to wink at Chloe as he clapped Mack on the shoulder. "Rory wants to know if this newspaper article's gonna interfere with game night?"

"It shouldn't," Mack muttered, rolling up the window, before slowly turning the cruiser around.

In the rearview mirror Mack saw Red, hands on bony hips, staring and grinning until Geneva came out of the house with an empty basket and gestured for him to finish helping her.

"Who's Rory to you, and what's game night?" Mack found the closeness of Chloe's voice discomfiting.

"They have nothing to do with the job."

"Everything has to do with the job. Remember the sheriff's given me *carte blanche.*" She pulled a sheet of paper out of her backpack. "If you want to see a printout of the e-mail in which Sheriff McQuire's given the go-ahead…"

"You e-mailed the sheriff on his honeymoon?" Mack applied the brake too heavily as he came to the end of the Whistling Meadows drive.

Chloe clutched the dashboard. "It's the least-invasive way to clear things up. He didn't have to answer."

But he would, Mack thought sourly, turning onto the county road. Because both Garrett and Samantha would think putting Mack out there was the best way for him to re-socialize. Well, they didn't understand that after a tour of duty in a war-torn hellhole, life wasn't so simple. People weren't what they appeared. And the man who didn't guard his back at all times was a fool. And worse.

"So who's Rory to you, and what's game night?" Chloe persisted, shaking her e-mail printout for emphasis.

Let her stew a bit.

Mack drove the short distance to Sarah Culpepper's under a sky as dark as his mood. "Rory's my godson," he replied at last, pulling into Miss Sarah's yard. Dust devils flecked with leaves roiled in the dirt. "Fridays we hook up for pizza and Nintendo Wii." And no, the reporter wasn't invited.

He got out of the cruiser. "I'll be right back."

Through the windshield, Chloe followed Mack's retreating form. What would she have done if he'd actually looked at the "e-mail" from Sheriff McQuire and read, instead, a library printout of her overdue books?

So what about Rory? A godson? Go figure. If she were to single out a particular person as a child's godparent, it would be someone a tad warmer than the deputy. She'd seen him in action with the kids at the high school. All cool, no-nonsense authority. Not an ounce of humor or playfulness. She'd love to see him caught up in Wii.

She might be able to finagle an invitation through Red Harris. He seemed friendly.

Before she could make a coded note to follow up, Mack returned. "Ms. Culpepper's not here. Sometimes my mother and father take her up to the house with them." He flipped open his phone.

"You're not going to check in person?"

"Only if they need me." He called but got no answer. Slowly, he put away his cell.

"It'll be okay," she said. "It's not as if you're bringing me home to 'meet the parents.'" She batted her eyes in mock flirtation.

He didn't answer. Instead, he drove up another long dirt road that abutted the Culpepper property. Freshly planted rows of something Chloe couldn't easily identify lined one side of the drive while hundreds of gnarled apple trees rose on the other, their blossoms blowing off in the wind. The horizon had turned an ominous pea-green.

"What were those seedlings?" she asked, getting out her notepad.

"Why do you ask?"

Because she didn't like the looks of that sky. And whenever she was nervous—or frightened, or overwhelmed—she retreated to her security blanket, the gathering of facts.

"Do your parents have a storm shelter?" she

asked, ignoring his question. She didn't want to be caught in a storm unprotected. To risk revealing a soft underbelly of fear to the deputy.

Mack sped up as a farmhouse in the middle of four huge oaks came into view. A woman stood at the open front door, waving frantically.

The hail began before Mack had a chance to turn off the engine. Large icy chunks clattered on the roof of the cruiser and bounced on the ground around them. The downpour quickly became so dense it almost obscured the woman in the doorway.

"I—I'm staying right here," Chloe breathed.

"No, you're not," Mack snapped over the increasing noise. "It's too dangerous. Open the door and run toward my mother."

When Chloe stepped outside the cruiser, the hail hit her like buckshot. She froze, then felt a jacket thrown over her head. Mack hauled her toward the house.

"My backpack!" she cried.

"Leave it!" He nearly threw her up the steps and into the farmhouse. Inside, the wet jacket fell on the floor. The hail on the farmhouse tin roof sounded like a Broadway audition for *Stomp*.

"Hurry!" His mother pulled her through the house before she even had a moment to wipe the hair from her eyes. "Funnel clouds have been spotted outside Brevard."

Mack urged Chloe down a flight of stairs. Somewhere a window broke. With a bang, he pulled the basement door shut behind them. "Is Miss Sarah with you?" he asked.

"I'm here." Sarah Culpepper's worried voice could barely be heard over the storm. "Though I don't know where Buster is."

When Chloe was able to catch her breath, she took in a dimly lit and rough-hewn room with shelf upon shelf of home-canned fruits and vegetables lining one of the walls. Sarah, wrapped in an old quilt, sat on one of two plank benches in a far corner of the room away from all that glass. A couple more quilts, a radio and several flashlights were on the bench by her side.

"Where's Pop?" Mack asked.

"In Asheville. Getting a part for the—"

"Cover yourself up," Mack cut her off as he grabbed a quilt and handed it to her. He handed Chloe the remaining one. "And turn your faces to the wall. In case."

Chloe didn't need to be told that "in case" meant flying debris. Praying it wouldn't come to that, she draped the quilt over her head and around her shoulders.

"Ms. Whittaker," she said before she turned her face to the wall, "how did you know we were coming?"

"I'm a mother, dear," the woman replied from her quilt cocoon.

Above them, they heard a tremendous thunderclap, then a crack and a hiss. Seconds later, the lights went out.

"Move over," Mack ordered, sliding onto the bench next to Chloe.

"Do you have a quilt?" She reached out to pat him.

"None left."

"Here, share mine." She fumbled in the dark to throw a corner of hers over his bulk as the whole house seemed to vibrate and a couple hundred canning jars knocked against one another on the shelves.

"Cover your damned head," he growled, pulling her roughly to his side and shielding her against his chest.

"Mind your language," Sarah snapped as glass shattered nearby on the basement floor.

"I do hope that's not the rhubarb sauce I just put up," Mack's mother fretted.

Chloe was glad for Mack's steady heartbeat against her ear. It helped to regulate the wild fluctuations of her own. With his strong arms wrapped around her, she couldn't help but think everything would turn out okay. Even if she did end up with the mark of his badge permanently imprinted on her cheek.

As the minutes—it seemed like hours—wore on, the pitch-dark and the close, earthy smell of the basement began to get to her. But every time she tried to surface for air, Mack wrapped her more tightly in the quilt.

"I...can't...breathe!" she protested. She struggled under the suffocating covering, but when she couldn't find an opening and her air supply seemed to have dwindled to nothing, she sank her teeth into the first bit of flesh her mouth encountered.

CHAPTER SIX

"ARE YOU CRAZY, WOMAN?" Mack glowered at Atherton, whose pupils were dilated in the glare of the flashlight his mother trained on them. "More to the point, have you had your rabies shots?"

Teeth marks circled the pad at the base of his thumb. Fortunately she hadn't broken the skin, or he would have driven her straight to the vet. "What were you thinking?"

"You were suffocating me with your big ol' arms around me!"

"Get a motel room," Miss Sarah cackled, switching on a second flashlight.

The creaking of timbers distracted him. The house was settling after its battle with the storm, which, as quickly as it had begun, had ended. Only going above would determine what kind of a storm it had been—hail only, wind shear or tornado—and the aftermath.

Glaring at his injured hand, he stood up.

His mother cleared her throat. He knew what was

coming. Now that the danger had passed, Southern manners would take over. "Mack, honey, I don't believe you introduced your friend."

She was not his friend.

"You don't know this is the reporter from the *Sun?*" Miss Sarah cut in. "I met her day before yesterday. She took pictures of Buster. I thought surely Mack would have brought her up to your place for supper by now."

That wasn't going to happen.

"I'm Lily Whittaker," his mother said to Atherton as she put down her flashlight to fold the quilts. "I sure gave you a fine welcome to my home."

"One I won't soon forget," Chloe replied. When she extended her quilt, her hand shook. "I'm Chloe Atherton."

Who, when it came to storms, wasn't quite as tough as she made out. And before Mack could stop himself, he began thinking of her not as Atherton, but as Chloe.

"She loved my hermit bars," Miss Sarah declared. "Wanted the recipe for publication, but it's a family secret."

"I made pecan sandies this morning," his mother said quickly. "A secret Whittaker-family recipe." Mack knew a taste-off was forthcoming. "Let's go above and see if anything's left of them." His mother swept the basement with her flashlight, then sighed heavily. "Those *were* jars of my rhubarb sauce that broke. Three, by the looks of it. Mind y'all's step now."

Cautiously Mack climbed the basement stairs, the women behind him. When he opened the door to the kitchen, he discovered a tree branch had broken the window over the sink. Wet debris covered the countertops and floor. Although brilliant sunshine now poured into the room, the air smelled acrid.

"Looks like we have our work cut out for us." Miss Sarah headed directly for the broom closet.

As his mother moved through the other rooms, checking for further damage, Chloe stepped toward the back door.

"Don't go outside," he warned. "The power's off. There may be lines down."

"But I want to get my backpack. Check my camera." She parted the flowered curtains to view the farmyard. "Look," she said in awe.

Standing behind her, he saw a white landscape. Layers of hail, some stones the size of golf balls, covered the yard, the farther fields and the orchard. The apple-tree branches were now bare. The vegetables, some recently planted, might survive, but with the blossoms ripped from the trees, there would be no fruit. Mack's heart sank. Produce wasn't a hobby for the Whittakers. It was income his parents counted on.

"It has a strange beauty," Chloe said.

"Not to a farmer."

She turned to study him thoughtfully.

"I need to get on the radio to headquarters," he

said before she could offer up pity or even understanding. "See whether this was an isolated cell or if
we have a county-wide disaster on our hands. I'll
bring you your backpack."

"But you said there might be downed lines."

"Mack knows what to do," his mother said, returning to the kitchen. "You stay with us. With the power
off, someone has to help drink up the milk with those
pecan sandies."

He didn't like leaving Chloe to chat over milk
and cookies with these two women. They'd
dangled single women in front of him more than
once. He didn't know if Chloe was single, in a relationship or married, but his mother and Miss
Sarah would know before he could even radio
headquarters.

"Another headache?" his mother asked, smooth-
ing his furrowed brow.

He pulled away from her touch. "Any damage in
the other rooms?"

"Not that I could see," she replied, clearly hurt.
"But I didn't check the attic. The hail most likely
wreaked havoc on the roof."

And now the crop that would have paid for a
new one was ruined. Keeping his parents afloat
was one of the reasons he'd joined the army
reserves in addition to his law-enforcement work.
Yet his paycheck was getting stretched thinner and
thinner.

Chloe was monitoring this exchange with interest. Time to head outside. When Mack opened the kitchen door, hail skittered across the floor from the back stoop in much the same way he felt daily events skittering out of his control. If he was to cope, he'd better find a few private moments to touch base with his AA sponsor.

Left in the kitchen with Lily and Sarah, Chloe felt as if she'd been foisted off once again, but the circumstances didn't warrant her calling the deputy on it. "Let me help," she said to the two women who were getting more cleaning supplies out of the closet.

"No," Lily replied. "You're company."

"I beg to differ," Chloe countered. "When you've seen someone's basement, you're no longer a guest."

The two women laughed.

"The child's right," Sarah said, handing Chloe a dustpan and a fox-tail brush. "Top to bottom's my cleaning motto. Begin with the counters, but be careful of broken glass."

Setting a box of extra-strength trash bags on the kitchen table, Lily rummaged in her pocket. Coming up with a cell phone, she extended it to Chloe. "Do you need to call home to see if your folks are all right?"

"N-no. They're in Atlanta. But thank you."

"I admire how tough you young women are." Sarah stopped sweeping and leaned on the broom.

"I lived all my life within five miles of my kin. Couldn't imagine any other way."

"Maybe she has family in the area," Lily suggested. "Do you?"

"No." Chloe concentrated on scooping glass, melting hail and broken twigs from the counter into the dustpan. She wanted to steer talk away from herself, but without her notepad, tape recorder or camera, she was at a loss as to how to redirect the conversation. "It's just me."

"Any brothers or sisters back in Atlanta?" Sarah asked.

This was the part that always required Chloe to inhale deeply and steel herself to utter one deceptively simple word. "No."

Lily waited, holding a trash bag under the dustpan that Chloe—frozen—held in her hand. "Clearly, we're making you uncomfortable with all our questions. We'll stop pestering you."

Chloe forced her hand to dump the contents of the dustpan into the outstretched trash bag. "Y-you're not—"

"Lily's not going to stop," Sarah said with a twinkle in her eye, "until she's asked you one more question. Are you married?"

"I'm not going to ask her that!" Lily protested.

"Only because I asked it for you." Sarah looked Chloe in the eye. "Are you married?"

That was an easy one. "No."

The door opened, saving Chloe from any need to elaborate. At the sight of Mack, his mother's face lit up. "How bad is it outside?" she asked.

Handing Chloe her backpack, he appeared surprised to see her with her sleeves rolled up.

"The hail dinged the cruiser pretty bad. But it's all cosmetic," he said, turning slowly to his mother, his eyes lingering on Chloe. "The same tree that broke this window took out the electrical wires to the house. I called the power company. The roof on the house looks okay, but the barn's sustained considerable damage."

"Oh, no. Your father's equipment…"

"As soon as possible, I'll help him get a tarp on the roof."

"What about the rest of the county?" Chloe asked, checking in her backpack. Fortunately nothing had been harmed.

"Kim Nash says the storm system has moved east. In its wake there's hail damage. Funnel clouds hopscotched across the county. So far no reports of touch-down, but in patches of the national forest the tops of the trees are sheared off."

"You have to go, of course," Lily said. "We'll be fine here."

Mack frowned. "Chloe's coming with me. Her article's about the work I do. And there's plenty of work out there."

His declaration, especially with his use of her first

name, nearly bowled Chloe over, but before he could change his mind, she grabbed her camera.

While Sarah, briskly sweeping the floor, chuckled softly, Mack's mother said, "I'll put some pecan sandies in a sack and some milk in a thermos."

Mack barely let his mother kiss his cheek. What was wrong with him?

"Now which night are you free to come for supper?" Lily asked Chloe.

"I—I don't know," she stammered. Family togetherness wasn't her thing. "I'll have to check my schedule of interviews and get back to you through Mack."

Mack looked at her as if she'd grown a third eye.

Chloe accepted the bag of cookies and the thermos of milk from his mother and stowed them in her backpack. She slung her camera around her neck, gave Sarah a quick wave, then opened the door to make her way carefully over the hail-strewn yard to the patrol car.

"Are you okay?" Mack asked, right on her heels.

"Sure," she replied. Trying for nonchalant, she aimed her lens at the white landscape. "It's obvious your mother's extremely proud of you." She turned the camera on him.

In the viewfinder his eyes were so dark they appeared black. "Sometimes it's kinder if your parents never know the truth." His head disappeared as he got into the car.

She caught her breath. Sometimes the truth, with

all its pain, was impossible to hide. "From what I've been told," she said, sliding in and trying to add to the conversation a lightness she didn't feel, "everyone in town thinks you hung the moon."

He gripped the steering wheel. "Do you believe everything you're told?" Hail crunched and popped under the tires as he drove across the farmyard.

"Usually when everyone's telling me one thing," she replied, "I'm standing on my head, looking for the flipside."

"That's what I was afraid of." Pulling the cruiser to a stop beside the defoliated apple orchard, he shook his head. "God, they never catch a break."

"Who?"

"My parents."

"I don't know much about farming," she said, safely back in reporter mode. Dealing with facts. "But do they have crop insurance?"

"No," he replied wearily as he pulled away. "Let's check on Miss Sarah's property."

Surprisingly, by the time they arrived at the main road, there was scant evidence of hail and almost no storm damage. It had rained heavily, yes, but not much more. Robotically Mack called his mother to let Sarah know everything at her house appeared okay, and that Buster was curled up under the rocker on the porch.

"What now?" Chloe asked, hoping that the man who'd cared enough to protect her from falling debris back in the basement would show up. The man who'd been outraged at the bite she'd inflicted. The man who showed a spark of warmth, whether kindness or anger.

But the man she got was cold and distant. "We listen to the radio and we drive around. You take pictures."

The damage was spotty. It could be severe on one side of the road and untouched on the other. Typical. Less than a mile down the road, they found a motorist who needed a hand. The man had been driving a pickup truck and went off the road into the ditch. Another motorist had stopped to help, but with only one person to drive and one to push, the truck was still stuck. Mack pulled to the side of the road. When he got out of the cruiser, he didn't say a word, didn't look back, so Chloe got out, too. Got behind the bed of the stranded truck and pushed with the two men until she thought the veins in her forehead might pop. After considerable rocking and even more cursing, they were able to free the pickup.

When Mack and Chloe returned to the patrol car, he seemed almost surprised to see her.

On the road again, she daubed at the mud on her pants with a tissue and hazarded a tough question. One she'd been wanting to ask for a long time now. "What effect has your service in Iraq had on your work?"

He didn't answer.

For reasons she couldn't explain, she didn't press.

Was it because of the discomfort she'd felt when June, Lily and Sarah had tried to get personal?

The day unwound with myriad tasks, big and small. Freeing more cars from ditches, removing downed branches from roadways, checking on elderly residents, making dozens of phone calls, directing traffic around trouble spots, rescuing escaped farm animals and ferrying people without power to the high-school gym where a temporary shelter had been set up.

Mack got a call from the dispatcher midafternoon. Kim gave him an address and a list of supplies he should deliver there. Main Street had been untouched by the storm, so Mack stopped at the Piggly Wiggly. They bought a cooler, some ice, food staples. When asked if he wanted to put it on the department tab, he shook his head. Took cash from his wallet.

In silence he and Chloe drove across the train tracks on the same road he'd taken the first night she was in town. He pulled to a stop in front of the same tired house. "Stay in the car." The way he said it brooked no disagreement.

He lugged the heavy cooler and a couple of full grocery bags up the front steps. A child, a toddler, let him in the front door.

In a few minutes, Mack was back in the car. Without explanation.

Who lived here? And what was the connection to

Mack? Chloe felt conflicted. Should she pursue the matter? Or was it something best left untouched like the Whittaker-family dynamics? How much of Mack was a legitimate story, and how much of the story was an invasion of his privacy?

Her editor claimed secrets were not what couldn't be known, but what couldn't be acknowledged.

After their own family tragedy, Chloe's mother always said the truth stays independent of hurt or help.

Around six in the evening when all they'd had to eat were the pecan sandies Lily Whittaker had given them, Chloe began to feel woozy. Part of a group of people who were filling sandbags in the parking lot of the sheriff's office in case the creek that ran behind Main Street should rise even farther, she put out her hand to steady herself against the brick building. Felt herself sinking.

Mack caught her before she fell. "I'm taking you back to June's."

"I just need something to eat. I'll go next door to the diner."

"You need more than food. You need rest. I'm driving you to the bed-and-breakfast." His arm around her waist, he guided her to what she now considered her second home. The cruiser.

"It's only a couple blocks," she protested. "I can walk."

"Do I have to make a scene and carry you?" A glimmer of heat danced in his eyes.

"Okay, I'll take the ride." He opened the passenger door, and she practically fell inside. The interior smelled of dirt, sweat, motor oil and stale coffee. She wrinkled her nose. "Your car needs a good cleaning."

"That'll be the first thing on your agenda tomorrow morning."

"You wash your own cars?"

"Hey, this is a small county. We have a small budget."

Then it hit her. "You're asking me to work with you tomorrow?"

"Yeah."

"Wait!" She fumbled in her backpack for her tape recorder. "Let me get this on the record."

He actually chuckled, and she was disappointed, seconds later, to see the sign for June's B and B.

Stopping out front, he turned to her. "Go inside. Let June fuss over you. Type up your notes. Whatever. But get some rest. You've earned it."

"I didn't take any notes all day," she said in surprise. Normally at the end of the day her hand was cramped from living life in the third person.

The intensity of his gaze reminded her of the strength of his arms, the solid bulk of his chest, his warmth during the worst of the storm. "I'll pick you up at eight," he said.

"I'll be taking notes tomorrow."

"I consider myself warned," he said as he leaned across to open the passenger door. For an instant he was so close the hair on the top of his head tickled her chin. His scent was masculine and very real and threatened to break through her detachment.

"Get going," he ordered, sitting upright again. His voice was rough but no longer forbidding.

She stepped out onto the sidewalk with the un-nerving realization that after her article was done, she'd still want to learn more about Mack Whittaker.

Mack resisted the urge to get out of the car and help Chloe as she stumbled up the steps of the B and B. She wouldn't appreciate his help. Stubborn woman. Yesterday at this time he'd wanted to throttle her. Run her out of the county for being a tabloid bottom-feeder. Today…he didn't know what he wanted.

He did know how good she'd felt in his arms. In the middle of a storm. In his parents' basement.

He shook his head. He was losing it. Or was he? For the time they were huddled under the quilt—he glanced down at his thumb where the teeth marks were beginning to fade—until she'd bitten him, there was nothing but an elemental human connection. Physical touch. Without words. Without expectations. Without complications. Without a future or a past…

He headed toward Tanya's house. When he'd de-livered the cooler and supplies earlier in the day, she'd said the baby had banged his head on an end table during the storm. The two middle kids, cooped up after being sent home from school early, were driving her nuts. He'd give her a break for a couple of hours. Play with the kids. Give them baths. Read them a story. Put them to bed.

Although it was painful being around children.

Tanya met him at the door, dark circles under her eyes. "God, I'm glad you came back," she said, leading him into the small living room dimly lit with battery-powered camp lanterns. "My sister called. She has electricity. If, right now, I was given only one wish, it'd be to put my feet up and watch a whole TV show, start to finish, without someone needing something from me."

"Go. Watch *two* shows," he said, pushing her to the door as Emma, Pete and Wayans plowed into him with glee. "Is Duke home?"

"Staying next door with his buddy J.D. tonight."

Mack tried not to let the relief show. He could handle Duke's rebelliousness. But he could barely handle the fact that the boy was growing up to be the spitting image of his father.

"You kids listen to Mack," Tanya admonished as she shrugged into a light jacket.

"Yes'm!" the three shrieked in unison, turning his pockets inside out, looking for candy.

"I don't know what I'd do without you," Tanya said, blowing him a kiss and heading out the door

He did. Without him, she wouldn't be in such a mess. Every day was a struggle for her. Because of him.

He shrugged off his morbid thoughts to turn his attention to Emma, Pete and Wayans. He loved kids.

Not, however, the same way he had before he'd gone to Iraq. Still, he could play a credible bucking bronco, make an edible PB&J, give three baths without flooding the bathroom, then tell a whopper of a bedtime tale. By the time Tanya came home, the kids were asleep, the dishes washed and in the drainer, and he'd repaired the lock on the back door.

"Thank you," she said, leaning against the kitchen counter. "You want a soda?"

Did her eyes ask if he wanted something more? He couldn't read signals anymore. Didn't have the desire to relearn them.

"No, nothing for me. I've had a long day, and it's not over yet."

"How's that thing with the reporter going?"

"She's only half a pain in the ass." Now why had he said that? It was unkind. And it wasn't true. The woman had shown herself vulnerable today. And then she'd shown herself to be strong and full of heart.

"Call me if you need anything," he said to Tanya.

"Like another pair of hands?"

"You can count on mine."

"I do."

Her trust unnerved him.

All the way back to the barracks, where he planned to catch forty winks, then hit the road again on patrol, he thought about Tanya. And Nate. His parents.

Then there was Chloe.

Working her way under his skin.

CHAPTER SEVEN

"THAT'S NOT A NEWS ARTICLE," Deirdre Kinkaid said. "That's blatant hero-worship."

Sorry she'd mentioned yesterday's events at all, Chloe held her phone to her ear as she searched under the inn's bed for her shoes. The storm had taken out the power at the *Sun*'s offices in Brevard, but Chloe would have much preferred the annihilation of a cell-phone tower. In particular, the one that serviced her editor.

"Deirdre, I'm not setting Mack Whittaker up as a hero. In the wake of the storm, the entire department pulled together heroically. I happened to be riding with Whittaker." Who was supposed to have picked her up fifteen minutes ago.

"Remember your unbiased observation. Your—"

"*Gravitas*, I know." She found one very muddy penny loafer, then the other. Poor June hadn't given even a peep of concern for her floors when Chloe had dragged in last night, disheveled and dirty. She stuck the shoes in a plastic Piggly Wiggly bag. She'd take them out to the backyard later and see if she could clean them. Today she'd have to wear her black lace-ups. "You don't have to hold my hand through this assignment," she told her editor.

"I hope not. The article isn't for the Living section. We're not looking for warm and cuddly here."

"What if the truth is warm and cuddly?"

"Now I know you're trying to tick me off."

Chloe heard a knock at her door. Would Mack come up to her room to get her? If so, things certainly had changed from yesterday.

"My ride's here. Gotta go."

She opened the door, not to Mack, but to June Parker.

"Sorry to bother you," June said, "but Mack is waiting for you downstairs."

"I have to find my shoes."

"Don't hurry. I put him in the parlor with a cup of coffee and a plate of biscuits." June delicately picked a minuscule piece of lint off her sweater sleeve. "How is…the article going?"

Chloe peered up from tying her shoe. "I think it's going okay. Though I'm sorry it took the storm to get it on track."

"Sometimes adversity brings out the best in us. And…sometimes it's nice there's someone to chronicle the best in us when we can't see it for ourselves."

Chloe looked directly at her hostess. "What, specifically, are you trying to tell me?"

June flashed a Cheshire cat smile. "Oh, it's a new day. And I often get to pondering after I've had my first cup of Earl Grey. Think nothing of it."

Right. What did people want to tell Chloe about Mack, but felt they couldn't? Not directly, at least. Chloe grabbed her backpack to follow June downstairs. Then the inn owner headed for her guests in the dining room and Chloe turned toward the front parlor.

Mack sat sprawled in a chair too small for him, his head thrown back, sound asleep. Coffee and biscuits sat untouched on a nearby table. The man probably hadn't slept more than a couple of hours last night. If at all.

Deirdre Kinkaid would not like the emotion that welled up inside Chloe. It was one of those *ahhh* feelings better left to photos of kittens and teddy bears with hats. And strong men with the least show of vulnerability.

When she stepped forward, the heart-pine floorboards creaked and he woke up with a reflexive jerk. He narrowed his eyes as if he was struggling to recognize her.

"Mack?"

"I was last I looked," he said, wincing as he massaged his arm. "Come on. The cruiser needs a bath." He looked at her feet. "You're going to ruin those shoes. You got any real boots?"

"No."

"We'll take care of that."

We was a promising word.

The day had dawned bright and clear with only the damp earth strewn with shredded leaves and the distant sound of chain saws to indicate there'd even been a storm the day before. Chloe knew, however, that not everyone was as lucky as those on Main Street.

"What's the damage update?" she asked.

"Power outages are still the biggest headache."

"How are your parents?"

"Doing okay." His evasiveness hinted the truth might be something else.

And then he did something strange. He opened the passenger door of the patrol car for her. She was shocked into silence.

He didn't speak, either, during the drive to Wal-Mart, where he led her to the hunting-and-fishing section and instructed her to try on, then purchase a pair of big black, rubber farm boots. Hands on hips, he stood in the parking lot until she put them on. Lord, the things were ugly. Was this some kind of practical joke?

The corner of Mack's mouth twitched. "Daisy Duke, you're not," he said. "But you're ready for the car wash."

Why did it sting that he thought she was unattractive?

As they hit the road again, she tried to get her thoughts back to business. "I've interviewed the other deputies," she began. "And you, of course. But can you tell me something about the sheriff?"

"The thing that tells the most about the sheriff is the department. Look at how it runs as a unit even when he's gone. That's testament to his work."

"I can see that," she said, irritated by his evasiveness and the fact that her backpack and now the enormous boots were reducing her legroom in the cruiser. "But what about the personality that drives the man?"

"Do you need to know that?"

"I do if I want the public to read an in-depth and compelling article and not just a dry essay," she said, starting to put her feet up on the dashboard.

"Hey, don't even think about it," Mack snapped, pointing at her oversize boots. At the self-service car wash, he pulled the cruiser into an empty bay on the end and cut the engine. When he looked at her, his expression was unreadable.

"What's Garrett like?" he said. "Let me put it this way. The honeymoon he's on makes the first two consecutive days of vacation he's ever taken."

"Wow," Chloe breathed. "His wife must be something."

"She is," Mack replied with such conviction Chloe wondered if he'd ever, at any time, had a romantic interest in the sheriff's wife. He plunked a roll of quarters in her hand before getting out of the car. "I'll wash. Your job is to feed the meter."

She clambered out of the passenger side. The boots made it impossible to move with any speed or grace. For a job this simple she had to dress like a goober? She had the feeling that Mack's tactic, after he'd resigned himself to letting her follow him, was to keep her off balance.

That only fueled her instincts to dig deeper.

"Heads up!" Mack said, grabbing the power-wash wand and aiming it at the car. Chloe blinked as a fine mist drifted in her direction, and he caught himself paying less attention to the car and more attention to her, standing in some odd, safari-type outfit, in boots that swamped her. Looking very, very appealing. She radiated a freshness, appeared grounded as if she lived in a world that was explainable, manageable. He'd like to live in that world.

Why had he brought her to the car wash this morning? It was part of a deputy's job, sure, but not a particularly important one. He could have let her sleep in after the work she'd done yesterday. Could have brought her to the courthouse later when he was scheduled to pick up and distribute the civil processes. She hadn't seen that yet. So why had he brought her along now?

Because he'd woken up this morning, wanting to see her.

"This thing is beeping already," she called out. "Do I feed it more money?"

"Yes." He hadn't even wet down the entire car yet. Only the front grille.

And she noticed. "Deputy Whittaker, you're not

making the most efficient use of county money. Shall we switch jobs?"

"Right," he replied, making broad sweeps with the wand. "As if you'd know what to do. When was the last time you washed that car of yours?"

"Never. It's a form of conservation. Very forward-thinking."

Having fed the meter, she grabbed a long-handled brush from a hook on the bay wall and began to scrub at resistant spots of mud. Her strawberry-blond hair had gone curly with the humidity and a lock dangled over one eye. She blew at it, but kept on scrubbing. What would it be like to kiss those lips now puckered in concentration? What kind of woman would she be in bed?

Bossy.

He chuckled.

"What's so funny?"

"Nothing." Especially if Garrett came home to find his deputy-in-charge had bedded the investigative reporter. "Here, you missed a spot. And the coin machine's beeping again."

"Why do I get the feeling I'm doing all the work?" she groused, popping six quarters into the machine.

"Because I'm in charge."

The sudden flare of her nostrils spoke volumes. She did *not* relish being subordinate. He thought back to her reaction to the storm when they were in his mother's basement. Apparently she didn't like events out of her control either. Who did? But what was *ever* under your control? he thought cynically.

"The least you could do is answer some questions."

"Okay." Her questions were probably safer than his wandering thoughts. "Shoot."

"When did you first want to follow a career in law enforcement?"

"Don't all boys grow up playing cops and robbers? I guess I never stopped."

"Did you play with Garrett McQuire when you were kids?"

"Since third grade. You could say we were inseparable."

"That's why you're his son's godfather."

"Yup."

"Did he play sports with you in high school?"

"No. He worked pretty near full-time after school from the minute he was old enough to get a permit."

"Ah. A workaholic from an early age."

No. Simply trying to stay out of his foster parents' way. Trying to earn something he could call his own.

She stopped scrubbing. "Did the sheriff go to Iraq, too?"

"No." Even though the water was still running, Mack shoved the power-wash wand into its holder. "The outside's clean enough. I'm going to drive the car over to the vacuum station. I brought old towels. You can dry. I'll get the inside."

He got in the cruiser and pulled out of the bay. In

the rearview mirror he could see her watching. Could sense the gears in that quick brain of hers clicking.

Well, he wasn't going to talk about Iraq. Not with her. Not with anybody. That place was relegated to the other side of the globe. And his nightmares.

Now he knew how to control any rogue thoughts of Chloe and him between the sheets. All he needed to do was remind himself she was hardwired to probe for answers. With someone like that, he'd never find peace.

At the vacuum station, he began excavating fast-food wrappers from the car. He could hear the clop-clop of boots as Chloe approached, but he didn't look up. Not even when he could sense her standing right behind him.

"Why don't you want to talk about your service experience?" she asked softly.

God, the woman didn't let up.

Clutching two fistfuls of trash, he stalked to the trash can and unloaded the wrappers before unhooking the vacuum hose. "How many quarters do you have left?"

She brought over the remaining coins, then stood facing him.

"What do you want from me?" he asked, unable to keep the growl from the back of his throat. "My army tour has nothing to do with my job in the sheriff's department. So leave it alone."

"Folks around here look up to you." As she spoke, she placed the quarters in his hand. One at a time.

Deliberately. Underscoring each sentence. "In part because you didn't shirk your duty when called. The respect makes your job run more smoothly."

"That's what you think, huh?"

"Unless you tell me otherwise." Having placed the last coin in his hand, she stared at him, studying him. His palm felt hot where she'd touched it. "If you have medals, I assume you received an honorable discharge."

"I did." Although no one was ever going to convince him he deserved one.

When he broke eye contact to jam quarters into the machine, Chloe knew she'd been shut off. Apparently she'd pushed Mack too far. And again his war experience had been the line in the sand. Deirdre would tell her to use sources outside Colum County to find answers, but Chloe didn't know. She just didn't know. Maybe her mantra about facts and information wasn't powerful enough to push her into another's obvious pain.

For the past fourteen years, she'd kept people at bay when they'd wanted to know more about her than bare-bones statistics. For the first three years out of college, she'd checked other people's copy for errors before the *Sun* sent the articles to print. She didn't get close to her coworkers. Not emotionally. For the past two years, she'd written articles on seasonal plants, on drought conditions, on garden-club meetings, all the while thinking she wanted to get out and write about meatier issues. But meatier issues meant asking tough questions that she wouldn't want asked of herself.

Coming up against a man very much the same, she had her first doubts about her chosen career.

She took one of the towels stacked on the back seat and began to dry the exterior. She finished in silence. As she sat with the passenger door open and exchanged the ugly rubber boots for her shoes, she didn't even listen to the conversation Mack was having with the dispatcher on the two-way radio.

Finally turning his attention to Chloe, he simply said, "We need to stop back at headquarters before picking up the processes at the courthouse."

"Can I get something to eat? I left June's without breakfast."

She expected him to snap at her. He didn't.

"You can go upstairs to the staff kitchen while I take care of some business with Nash." Although his voice was flat, there was a hint of relief. Relief that she wouldn't be hanging around for this particular transaction?

She didn't push the issue. Instead, on the ride back to Main Street, she tried to sort out the thrust of her article. A clear story arc. Trouble was, this was her fourth day in town, and her thoughts were still jumbled and her notes of little use. If Deirdre asked for her copy now, Chloe could write up a description of the sheriff's department, complete with history, duties, personnel descriptions and impact on the community. But that wasn't the real story.

The real story was Deputy Mack Whittaker, but he wasn't giving it up.

Back at headquarters, she left him talking to the dispatcher while she climbed the stairs to the kitchen. Deputy Rollins sat at the central table. He'd been introduced as the rookie on the force, although he looked maybe ten years older than Chloe.

Glancing up from his newspaper, he nodded in greeting.

From the sidebar, she got a cup of coffee, a container of yogurt and a banana, then sat beside him.

"You know," he said, lowering the paper, "I've been trying to place you. The name Atherton rings a bell."

"Well, I didn't grow up around here." She licked the peeled-off yogurt lid.

"Me, neither. I'm from Atlanta."

Chloe froze with her tongue halfway out.

"Wh-what brings you to the mountains?" she managed to ask, steering the conversation to him.

"My wife," he replied, giving Chloe one long, final look before shaking his head. "She wanted to raise our kids on some land with a garden, a dog and chickens."

"How's that working out?" She made herself nonchalantly stir the yogurt with her plastic spoon.

"Not too good. Word traveled fast that my wife is a soft touch. We have seven dogs now. All of them dropped off on different occasions in the dead of night on our front porch. I'm going broke with neutering fees."

Chloe breathed more easily now that the conversation had turned from her. "There's a special place in heaven for your wife. But how about you? The job treating you okay?"

"Sure is. I don't feel like a cog in a wheel the way I did in the city. Because I'm not always pulling double shifts, I have more time to work on my songs."

"You're a songwriter?"

"You can catch my act on Saturday at the Pillar and Post. Have Whittaker bring you."

The idea of Mack out for a night of fun was a thought hard to get her mind around. "Do you see him much after-hours?" she asked.

"Atherton, time to leave!" Mack's voice boomed from the head of the stairwell. A blanket-wrapped bundle tucked under his arm, he looked as if he'd overheard them. And didn't approve of what he'd heard.

"Atherton," Rollins murmured. "About a dozen years ago there was a sad story in the *Atlanta Journal Constitution* about a family named Atherton. A real tragedy—"

Chloe stood up so quickly she tipped her chair over. Rollins righted it.

"Can we get going?" Mack asked impatiently.

Yes. Please.

She shot a wave at Rollins, then headed for the stairs.

"I don't like you pumping my coworkers for information about me," Mack growled as he pushed her outside. "In fact, I don't like you poking around in my personal life, period."

She knew how he felt, but she said, "Is that why I'm back to *Atherton?*"

He fairly threw the bundle he carried into the trunk.

"What is that?" she asked.

"A delivery Nash needs me to make."

"To whom?"

He leveled that cold-eyed gaze on her again. "To a family badly affected by the storm. You'll forgive me," he said acidly, "if I protect their pride by not divulging their identity."

Her nostrils flared on a sharp intake of breath. When Claire had died, the newspaper wasn't supposed to have printed Chloe's name because she'd been a minor. Only twelve years old. But someone got it wrong. Transposed the number to twenty-one. Printed her name. And unleashed even more grief on an already shattered family.

Clutching the cruiser's armrest until her knuckles went white, Chloe was grateful that Mack was brooding. She needed the silence to compose herself.

At the courthouse she followed Mack into the formidable brick building. "What are processes?" she made herself ask.

"Civil summonses. Criminal summonses. Domestic

violence orders. Driver's license pickup orders. Eviction notices. Subpoenas." Mechanically he reeled off the list. "Make an appointment with Judge Franklin. She'll be glad to answer any of your questions. She makes the decrees. I just serve 'em."

Well, if he wasn't going to give her even this cut-and-dried information, she'd have to keep her eyes and ears open. Maybe the deputy wasn't capable of thawing out. At least not in a week's time. Maybe she didn't want him to. If the department had to be the star of her article, after all, there was nothing wrong with a well-written civics lesson.

She followed Mack as he checked in, signed a ream of papers, then picked up the processes. He didn't introduce her to anyone. Back in the patrol car, he began sorting the legal forms.

"What are you doing?" she asked to keep her thoughts on work.

"I'm putting these in a delivery order. No need to waste gas running back and forth across the county." He came to one document and froze. "Damn! He's not going to get away with this."

"What?"

Mack slammed the car into gear and backed up, narrowly missing the big silver BMW in the spot marked *Judge Esther Franklin.*

As the deputy switched on the overhead flashing lights and charged out of the parking lot, the process he'd been reading slid onto the floor at Chloe's feet.

She picked it up. An eviction notice. It stated that one landlord, Frank Hudson, had begun proceedings to evict one tenant, Tanya Donahue, from his property.

CHAPTER EIGHT

MACK COULDN'T BELIEVE Frank would do this.

Turning off Main Street onto Williams, he pulled to a stop in front of the Hudsons' tidy bungalow. He left the lights flashing. He wanted Frank—and Frank's neighbors—to take notice. The man, dressed impeccably as usual in khakis and logoed golf shirt, was clearing the front yard of minor debris from the storm. He looked up at the commotion. And looked downright chagrined when he saw it was Mack getting out of the cruiser.

"I'm well within my rights," he protested as Mack strode across the lawn. "She's three months behind on the rent."

"Are we talking letter of the law or spirit?" Mack asked, planting himself in front of Frank and trying to keep his anger in check. "Have a heart. The woman's a war widow. With four kids. And no job."

Frank kept his rake between the two of them. Although his perfectly styled silver hair didn't budge in the breeze, the man himself looked ruffled. "And military benefits, I presume."

Mack clenched his fists at his side. "You can shove those so-called military benefits. They don't cover squat."

"Well, I have to look after me and mine," Frank said, glancing over his shoulder to where Lara Hudson's face appeared in an upstairs window. "My company downsized, and I was let go."

"Upper management, weren't you?" When Mack took another step forward, Frank dropped the rake and took two steps back. "I bet you walked away with a nice settlement."

"That's none of your business." Nervously Frank fiddled with his wedding ring. "Tanya's not the only one with a family to raise. Right now mine needs the income from my rental properties. I'm willing to forgive Tanya those three months, but I want her out so I can put someone in who can pay."

"You're going to throw her out on the street," Mack snapped, finding it more and more difficult to hold on to what scant patience he had left.

"Once the notice is served, she's got ten days," Frank offered in defense as he glanced toward the street. Traffic on Williams was slowing as people paused to look at the patrol car and its flashing lights. The confrontation on the lawn. "She has family," Frank insisted. "Her parents are here in town. Along with her sister. Her brother's in Brevard.

And what about the Donahues? They should be helping her."

For whatever reason, they hadn't so far. Mack had heard rumors the Donahues were struggling, too.

"Who is *she?*" Frank suddenly asked, pointing over Mack's shoulder.

Mack turned to see Chloe standing nearby and scribbling in her notepad. He'd totally forgotten about her. But why not use her to his—to Tanya's—advantage?

"Chloe Atherton," he declared, gesturing her closer, "is a member of the press."

"Why the hell did you have to bring the media into this?" Frank bellowed, waving his arms and finally disturbing his hair.

"She's here for the week. Doing an article on the department. You happened to be part of my job today."

"I shouldn't have been," Frank said directly to Chloe. "You make sure you take this down. Once the judge signs off on the eviction, the sheriff is sworn to deliver the notice to the tenant." He swung round to glower at Mack again. "The landlord isn't supposed to be *harassed.*"

"I'm not harassing you, Frank," Mack replied, lowering his voice. Aiming, if not for conciliatory, then for sane. "I thought we could talk, man to man." Although what kind of man could so easily toss a struggling family out of their home? "Maybe work something out that would show compassion to a widow and her fatherless children."

Lara Hudson stepped out of the house onto the front steps. Holding tightly to a hand towel, she didn't make an effort to come down into the yard.

"That's a low blow, and you know it," Frank fumed. "Tanya Donahue is going to be okay. If nobody else sees to it, you will."

Mack cut a sideways look at Chloe, who was recording this whole interaction. "I shouldn't have to see to it. Her problem wasn't a department issue until you made it one. Write that down," he said to Chloe.

"Write this down," Lara called out from the porch. "Deputy Whittaker is crazy."

Mack recoiled.

"He won't stop until he's personally saved every down-and-out soul in Colum County," Lara continued loudly as she hurried down the front steps to stand protectively in front of her husband. She spoke to Chloe, but turned a righteous glare on Mack. "He's making himself a long list. Started with the sheriff as a boy. Moved on to those illegal-alien kids at the high school. Then Burt Jones. Now he's added Tanya Donahue and her lot. But for all his so-called charity, Mack Whittaker sure has had a devil of a time saving himself."

Because what Lara said was more truth than lie, Mack bit his lip to keep from saying something he'd regret.

"Now," Lara continued, "having come out of his alcoholic haze, our deputy's forgotten he's supposed to execute the duties of his office on behalf of law-abiding citizens."

"Hush!" Frank growled, pulling Lara back.

"*Stop!*" Chloe stepped smack in the middle of the threesome. "Right now." She leveled a warning look first at Frank, then at Lara, then at Mack. "Is it true what Mr. Hudson said earlier?" she asked Whittaker. "That the landlord shouldn't be involved in the eviction process after the judge has signed off on it?"

"You bet it is!" Frank crowed. "I'm no liar."

"I asked the deputy." Chloe turned to him.

"Technically," Mack said. "But—"

"Then I won't be party to this." She stuffed her notebook in her pocket. "Whittaker, if you're not in the cruiser in two seconds, I'm calling for backup." She stalked down the walkway.

Mack saw red. Who the hell did she think she was?

"Who the hell do you think you are?" she shouted at him when he slid behind the wheel. "You *used* me! And for something illegal."

He quickly pulled away from the curb before Frank and Lara could dig out lawn chairs to watch the new show.

"I wasn't doing anything outside the law. I was trying to talk to Frank as a concerned citizen. Not as a deputy."

"Funny, but you're wearing a uniform and a badge. And your entrance, lights flashing and all, sure looked official."

"You can't begin to understand."

"Then tell me." She smacked the dashboard with the flat of her hand. "When I catch a glimpse of some truth, you shut down. Shut me out."

Staring straight at the road, he tried to shut her out now.

"Who is Tanya Donahue?" Damn, the reporter in her was relentless.

"Nate Donahue's widow."

"Come on, Whittaker. Don't make this like pulling teeth. Nate Donahue is…?"

"A reservist killed in Iraq."

"A buddy?"

"From high school, yeah."

"In your unit?"

"Right again." Without coming to a full stop, he pulled sharply out of Williams onto Main Street.

"You came home," she said, "and he didn't, and now you're trying to look out for his widow."

"Something like that." But nothing like that.

She crossed her arms and slid down in her seat. "Thinking about your friend's wife and kids thrown out of their home, I can see why you'd fly off the handle. But the guns-ablazing act was over the top."

"Are you going to write it up?"

"I don't know yet." Something about her seemed deflated.

"When will you know?"

"Can you let me off at June's?" she asked, her

voice tired and flat. "I don't have the stomach to be there when you issue Tanya the eviction notice."

"Sure." Royally pissed off at himself, he pulled in front of the bed-and-breakfast. He hadn't realized he appreciated the reporter's—no, the woman's... Chloe's—respect until it appeared he'd lost it.

CHLOE HAD SPENT MOST of the afternoon soaking in her room's enormous claw-foot tub while she'd gone over her notes and tried to decide whether to pursue the unfolding saga of Deputy Whittaker. Eventually she'd given up and headed to Rachel's Diner for supper.

She wished she hadn't. The diner, unlike during the day, was filled with families. Laughing. Joking. Catching a bite before Little League practice. Or ballet classes. Or just giving Mom a midweek break from cooking. Chloe withdrew into herself.

"Is something wrong with that chicken pot pie?" Coffeepot in hand, the diner owner stood over her.

"No." Chloe stopped pushing chunks of the entrée around in its ramekin. "It's delicious. But I don't have much of an appetite tonight."

Rachel looked skeptical, yet she moved on to the next table.

Chloe knew Mack didn't want her prying into his personal life—which, she noted, included another reference to alcoholism. But by confronting the landlord when he should have been serving the eviction notice to the tenant—all in front of a member of the press—Mack had blurred the lines between his own interests and those of the department, and had publicly opened the door for her to investigate.

And what about those interests? Was Tanya more than a friend in need?

Not digging into this whole side story might prove Chloe was indeed a lightweight in the news industry. Destined to forever cover weddings and garden parties. She did have something to prove. Not only to her editor, but to herself. Having confronted the truths in her own life, surely she could handle those of others. She didn't need to be ruthless, only thorough.

Paying her supper bill, she headed for her Yugo. And Tanya Donahue's house.

There was no mistaking the Donahue residence. In the fading evening light, Tanya Donahue sat on the front porch in an aluminum folding chair, holding a sleepy toddler while two elementary-school-age children ran around the front yard.

Chloe hadn't counted on the kids being up.

Putting aside her discomfort, she parked, climbed out and stood at the edge of the yard. "Hi." She waved as she hoisted one backpack strap over her shoulder. "I'm from the *Western Carolina Sun.* Could I talk to you?"

"News travels fast," Tanya replied, her voice a worn-out rasp. "Come on up."

When Chloe drew closer, she could see tear streaks in the woman's makeup. "Sorry. I only have this one porch chair, and Wayans has just settled down."

"That's okay," Chloe replied, noting Wayans was about the same age Claire had been. She quickly turned her attention to Tanya. "I can sit on the step."

"So you heard about the eviction notice."

"Y-yes." Chloe hesitated to correct Tanya's assumption that this visit was about her most recent difficulties.

"I bet there are hundreds of stories like mine all over the country," Tanya said, wiping her eyes. "That doesn't make mine any easier to accept."

"No." Chloe decided to let her talk.

"Especially when Frank Hudson has the first nickel he ever made." As Tanya carefully shifted her son in her lap, Wayans pursed his lips and rubbed his eyes, but didn't wake up. "I know Frank was laid off," Tanya continued in a lower voice. "But with the money he's pinched over the years, he could have retired when he was thirty."

Chloe wasn't interested in Frank Hudson. He was a minor character in this. Neither particularly bad nor good. And far from any real power source. "Where will you go?" she asked Tanya, instead.

"Even though it'll be a *really* tight fit, my sister says she'll take us in temporarily. Till I can find work. But any work I can get won't cover the child care I'll need." She inhaled with a shudder. "I haven't worked since high school. I loved staying home with our kids. Nate…loved coming home to us…"

"Tell me about Nate," Chloe said, looking at Wayans. Remembering Claire.

A fat tear rolled down Tanya's cheek and onto the head of her sleeping child. "God, he was a good man. He made me laugh. Something I don't do much these days."

Chloe looked down at her own hands. She wasn't in the Living section anymore. This was life. Real and raw. And exposed. The way it had been for her family fourteen years ago.

Tanya's other two children, a boy and a girl, ran up onto the porch, their fine brown hair plastered to their sweaty faces. "Mama, we're hungry," the girl said, lowering her voice as Tanya put her finger to her lips and nodded at the sleeping toddler on her lap.

"And thirsty," the boy added. "Can we have the stuff Mack brought over?"

"You can each have a juice box. And some string cheese or peanut-butter crackers, but no more cookies, y'hear?"

"Yes'm," the two mumbled as they dashed into the house.

"Growing kids," Tanya commented. "They come with hollow legs."

"I wouldn't know," Chloe replied in a near whisper, struggling to stay in the present.

"If it wasn't for Mack," Tanya continued, stroking Wayans's hair, "I don't know what I'd do."

"Wh-what about Mack?"

"He's always bringing food over. And I know he badgers the staff at the department to give up any clothes their kids have outgrown. When he's off duty, he'll keep an eye on my four so I can catch my breath. He fixes stuff around the house. He even helps with the bills but I didn't tell him about the rent. I know his paycheck runs thin fast, what with him trying to keep his parents' farm afloat."

"So Mack's a knight in shining armor," Chloe said. Lara Hudson had implied as much, although not kindly.

Tanya offered a wan smile. "Mack would hate you saying that, but to me he's been a godsend, yes. Although…"

"Although?"

As the mists of the April evening began to rise, a whippoorwill's plaintive call trilled in the distance.

"Don't get me wrong," Tanya said. "I should be the last person to say anything against Mack…but sometimes I worry about his motives."

Chloe leaned forward. "How do you mean?"

"There's something gnawing at him. Something dark. As friends, he and Nate went back a long way, and Nate's death hit him hard. But…it's almost as if Mack feels guilty."

"Did the army give you any information that would make you think that?"

"I was told Nate died when an insurgent—a suicide bomber—entered their tent. Mack was in the shower at the time."

"How could an insurgent get that close?"

"I don't know. And Mack isn't saying."

"Survivor's guilt is what that's called," Chloe said.

"Maybe. But…this is the bad part. The part that makes *me* feel guilty. I don't know what I would have done without Mack's help, and with him here, there's always a piece of Nate around, but…how can I explain this? It's been a year and a half that Nate's been gone, yet somehow Mack's brooding keeps me from moving on. Do you know what I mean? Sometimes it nearly suffocates me."

Chloe froze. Years ago she'd heard neighbors gossiping. One had claimed that Chloe's fixation on her sister's death had nearly destroyed her parents' marriage.

"I sound like a big ol' ingrate, and I'm not," Tanya said, waving a gnat away from her sleeping child. "But I've had a lot piled on me today. I guess I needed to unload." Sighing, she ran her fingers through her already tousled hair. "On someone who hasn't heard my story over and over."

Chloe rubbed her arms. "The night's gone chilly," she said. "I'd better go."

Her son in her arms, Tanya got up with difficulty.

"Sometimes I stand in my kids' bedroom doorway and watch 'em sleep. Glad someone can have a worry-free night."

"Mama! He's into the cookies!" one of the children called from inside the house.

The young mother sighed. "And so it goes."

Chloe held open the screen door for her. The house wasn't much of a shelter, but in ten days Tanya and her family would lose even that.

Just because the process Frank Hudson had followed was legal, did that make it right? And yes, Deputy Whittaker had crossed a line this afternoon, but did that make him wrong?

And what about the concerns Tanya had expressed about Mack, the man?

Chloe had read a lot about post-traumatic stress disorder. Perhaps Mack was suffering from it. Perhaps, too, she'd gotten herself in way over her head with this article. Especially since it was dredging up her own past.

Suddenly Chloe didn't want to be alone. Earlier in the day Deputy Hannah Breckinridge had mentioned she'd finish her shift at eleven tonight and had wanted to know if Chloe might like to join her for popcorn and a DVD. Although Chloe had never been one to foster gal pals, she headed for department headquarters. Because she wasn't going to get any sleep tonight.

AFTER AN EVENING OF helping his father gather supplies to repair the barn roof, Mack dragged himself back to headquarters with the single thought of a shower and bed. He didn't need to see Chloe sitting in the staff kitchen, laughing with his coworkers about to punch in for the graveyard shift. He rubbed his tired eyes to see if she was a mirage.

"Deputy Whittaker," she said.

"Are you waiting for me?"

"No. For Hannah. Breckinridge."

What could he say to that? He stood in the middle of the kitchen and scrutinized her as the other deputies pretended they weren't watching.

"But now that you're here," Chloe said, "I do have a couple requests since my time is running out in Applegate."

Three more days would bring them to Sunday. They were past the halfway point. He should feel better about that than he did. "Yes?"

"I understand surveillance begins on a fake lottery ticket—"

"No way." Following anonymous phone-in tips, he was to begin the operation tomorrow night with the graveyard. "You're not in on that."

"Why not?" Sooner asked. "Initial surveillance isn't particularly dangerous. We're just checkin' this guy out. It may not lead to anything."

"Surveillance is boring as hell," Darden chimed

in. "She can have my shift later in the week if she wants to stick around a few extra days."

"I'm going to be sitting in an unmarked vehicle all night," Mack protested. "And we're supposed to have a spring freeze."

"I'll wear long underwear," Chloe replied, as if throwing down a gauntlet. Was she still disappointed in him because of the dustup with Frank Hudson? His fellow deputies stood behind her, struggling not to smile.

"Up all night," he countered, "how do you expect to stay awake your last two days here?"

"Let me worry about that. There are only two more things I want to see…" She hesitated as if there might be more. "Surveillance and some deputy downtime."

"Deputy downtime?" Where he was concerned there was no such thing.

"Yeah," Darden said, heading for the stairs. "Those of us off Saturday night are going to see Rollins perform at the Pillar and Post. We checked the schedule, and you're not on duty. Stands to reason, you'll be taking Atherton."

She'd said downtime, not date night.

And after spending eight hours alone in a car with her?

He looked at Chloe, who still appeared cool and collected. As if the whole thing was no big deal. Hardly more than a couple of items to check off

her assignment list before she headed back to…
wherever it was she lived.

So why was he all hot and bothered?

CHAPTER NINE

AFTER A SLEEPLESS night filled with doubts and disconcerting thoughts that had sent him to a 6:00 a.m. AA meeting, Mack walked into Garrett's office to begin his day. Only to be faced with the object of his disconcerting thoughts.

Chloe.

Sitting at the sheriff's desk, she was pecking away on a laptop, her hair pulled haphazardly into a topknot stuck through with two pencils. Even he could tell that her knitted sweater vest and pants were way out of style. Why did she always wear such off-putting clothes? As if she didn't want anyone getting too close.

"What are you doing?" he barked.

She continued typing. "I'm looking up available apartments in the area."

Good God, she wasn't thinking of moving here, was she?

"For Tanya Donahue," she added, looking up at him. "When I talked to her last night, she said she'd be moving in with her sister. I thought she'd be more comfortable with a place of her own. So I'm seeing if social services or local charities might offer anything besides communal shelters."

He didn't know what ticked him off more. That this outsider thought Applegate couldn't take care of its own or...

He slammed the office door. "You talked to Tanya?"

Tenting her fingers under her chin, Chloe leaned back in Garrett's chair and eyed him with a great deal more equanimity than he felt. "Yes. You opened that door."

Damn. He could see needing another AA meeting later in his day.

"Did you ever stop to think," she asked, "that some media coverage might actually help Tanya?"

He saw stars as the beginning of a migraine made his right eye water. If he didn't get some caffeine in him stat, he was in trouble. "Did you ever stop to think how publicity could hurt the Donahue family?" he snarled.

"If you're getting a headache," she said, studying him intently, "apply pressure to the site. I get them, too."

Ignoring her advice—her meddling—he strode around the desk and pushed her chair, with her in it, aside. He remembered the conversation he'd overheard between her and Rollins, and used the search engine she'd been working with to look up "chloe atherton atlanta georgia."

"What are you doing?" she cried, struggling to regain possession of her laptop.

He didn't answer. Everyone had skeletons in the cyberspace closet. Some real. Some specious. The reporter needed to be shown the downside of free-wheeling investigation and unsubstantiated reporting.

He scrolled through the offerings that popped on the screen. Were the prominent CDC scientist or the adult-toys retailer or the Emory professor related in any way? And then he came to a listing for an old *Atlanta Journal Constitution* article. On the death of a toddler. Claire Atherton. The excerpt mentioned a police investigation involving an older sister, Chloe.

"No!" Chloe tried to push his hand away from the keyboard, but he'd already clicked to the full article.

When she saw there was no stopping Mack, Chloe rolled her chair into a very tight spot between a filing cabinet and a coatrack. Her heart pounding in her throat, she drew her knees to her chest. Sat by helplessly as he read the fourteen-year-old article.

She could still feel how bitterly cold it had been that day. See the frozen pond. Hear Claire begging to slide on the ice. Her mother had had a report due. Had asked Chloe to take Claire outside to feed the ducks. But the ducks had flown…

Feeling sick to her stomach, Chloe buried her face between her knees.

You must face what happened, she heard her mother say. *We must all try to move on.*

We still love you, her father had insisted.

But Claire was still dead.

"This was you?" a voice much closer to her asked. Mack's voice.

"Yes," she whispered into her knees.

"But it's a 1994 article. This Chloe is twenty-one."

"I—I was twelve. It was a mix-up. My name never should have been printed."

When he didn't say anything else, she looked up. Saw the shallow rise and fall of his breathing. Read accusation on his face.

"It was an accident," she offered in weak defense. Although if she hadn't taken her eyes off Claire for those few minutes... If she hadn't suggested hide-and-seek...

"I can see it was a terrible accident," he replied, stepping away from the computer. From her. "But what I can't see is why, with this tragedy in your life, you would choose a career of digging up the pain of others."

How could she explain?

Someone knocked on the office door, opening it at the same time. Deputy McMillan stuck his head into the room. "Sorry. But another tip just came in on that fake lottery scheme." He handed Mack a slip of paper. "Atherton, you don't look so hot. Didn't Whittaker at least offer you a cup of coffee?"

Chloe stood on shaking legs. "I need air," she said, pushing past the two men.

Outside, she followed the sound of running water to the creek behind headquarters. She stood at the edge of the parking lot by the guardrail, gazing down into the fast-moving stream, still swollen and muddy from the storm two days ago. Her thoughts felt like those waters.

How could she begin to explain the survival techniques, all involving facing reality head-on, that her analytical family had patched together?

She turned to sit on the guardrail and saw Mack walking across the parking lot, her backpack in hand.

"I was out of line back there," he said, his tone robotic. "I'm the last person who should question how someone else chooses to live her life." When he handed her the backpack, the look in his eyes said he had too many of his own ghosts to deal with. He didn't want to be saddled with hers. "I have to run to Brevard to pick up an office supply order. You riding along?"

"No," she replied quickly. "Hannah's doing a fire-safety talk at the seniors' center. I think I'll take that in."

"Suit yourself. But get some rest this afternoon before we meet back here at nine tonight."

She bunched her brows in question.

"Surveillance?" he added. "You still interested?"

"Y-yes." She dug deep for her lapsed detachment. "I need to see all aspects of the department."

As Mack walked away from her toward his patrol car, Chloe wondered if he wasn't a distorted mirror image of herself. The thought made her feel twelve again and defenseless.

"PAY ATTENTION!" RORY shouted as he swung the Nintendo Wii remote like a tennis racket.

"You pay attention," Mack returned. "To those pants of yours." He gave his thirteen-year-old godson's fashionably low-slung pants a tug while returning the serve. His "ball" lobbed into the "stands," hitting a "spectator."

"Hey! No messin' with my uni!" Rory protested, clutching his sagging pants and laughing. With the living-room rugs rolled up, the two were jockeying for position in front of the McQuires' television. "If you can't play fair, I'll have to get Red to take your place."

"No, thanks," the farm manager called from the Whistling Meadows kitchen where he was playing cards with Geneva. "I get enough exercise with my chores. I don't need to be standing in front of a TV screen, swinging at an imaginary ball. Used to be, you swatted at things that weren't there, they put you in the funny farm."

Rory served again before Mack could get his remote in the air. "Game! Set! Match!" the boy crowed.

This was Friday game night, something Mack knew Rory looked forward to every week, but Mack couldn't concentrate. The upcoming surveillance preyed heavily on his mind. Rory was beating him without even trying.

The teenager put down his handheld device to brush his floppy brown hair out of his eyes. "Maybe you're low on fuel," he said. "Let's go get some nachos."

Mack followed his godson into the kitchen where the boy put a bowl of cubed cheese and salsa into the microwave. Mack snagged a couple of tortilla chips while they waited for the concoction to melt.

"Two more days till Dad and Samantha get home," Rory said, hopping from foot to foot. "I can't wait. I want to know if they visited Nottingham and Sherwood Forest." He spread his long, skinny body horizontally along the counter, making Mack suspect the kid didn't have a bone in his body.

Geneva cleared her throat. "That counter is not a sofa," she warned.

Rory shot her a heart-melting grin and the hand sign for "I love you." The microwave dinged, and he bolted upright.

Mack was always amazed at how well-adjusted Rory was, despite the complications of his blended and extended family. The kid spent the school year with Garrett, his father, and vacations with Noelle, his mother, a banker now working in London, England. When Garrett and Samantha had decided to marry, they'd had Rory's wholehearted support. In turn, they'd chosen spring break in London for their wedding so that Rory could be best man and still spend time with his mother. Rory flew home when the sheriff and his bride set out for their honeymoon. A seasoned traveler at thirteen, the kid was as down-to-earth as they came.

Back in the day when he'd wanted kids, Mack had hoped for one like Rory.

"I said we're picking 'em up at the airport Sunday at one." Red had raised his voice to get Mack's attention.

"You going to be able to make the reception at the fire hall?" Geneva asked.

"I'll be there," Mack replied, although these days large crowds made him jumpy.

"Gin!" Geneva slapped her cards on the table, much to Red's disgust. "I hear that reporter who's been tailing you will be there. We're gonna have *coverage*."

"I hope it doesn't spook Samantha," Red groused, referring to the ugly week the paparazzi had spent camped out in Applegate trying to make a story out of the sheriff and the hotel heiress.

"She'll be cool," Rory said as he pulled the melted-cheese concoction out of the microwave and placed it on the table. "You should've seen her in London. We got to see the Duchess at work," he said, using Red's favorite nickname for Samantha. "Nothing got her flustered."

"Ah, love." Geneva sighed as she shuffled the deck of cards.

"More like a solid connection to law enforcement," Red remarked dryly. "Those media types learned not to mess with the sheriff."

"You'd pick up on that angle, you old fool," Geneva retorted, dealing. "You haven't an ounce of romance in you." Her words were tart, but the smile she bestowed on Red was sweet.

As Rory poured sodas for everyone, he winked at Mack. When the housekeeper had moved with Garrett and Rory to Samantha's farm, the farm manager had found a new kick in his step.

"Looks like you're the next one to walk down the aisle," Geneva said to Mack. The woman knew no boundaries. Unlike Red who, with the help of Samantha, had taken Mack in when he'd reached the lowest, most alcohol-drenched point in his life. Red knew not to push too far, and now he nudged Geneva under the table.

She ignored him. "I mean, aren't you the last un-attached deputy in the department?"

"That I am," Mack replied, putting a plate of cut-up veggies and the bowl of tortilla chips on the table next to the dip. "With no plans to change my status," he declared, plunking himself down in an empty chair and taking up Rory's unspoken challenge to see who could put away the most food the fastest.

"What about the reporter?" Geneva persisted. "I caught a glimpse of her. She's cute enough."

"You ever hear of conflict of interest?" Mack asked around a mouthful of cheesy chip. Tonight

Rory was beating him at food intake, too. "Any romantic involvement would look like I was trying to sway the outcome of her story."

"You're mighty sure of your persuasiveness." Geneva harrumphed. "Besides, if you were interested in the girl, well, this assignment isn't going to last forever." With a sly smile, Geneva surveyed the hand she'd dealt herself.

It made Mack uncomfortable to admit that thought had crossed his mind. On more than one occasion. But earlier today, when he'd crossed the line, her look of betrayal was an additional pain he didn't need.

He glanced at the clock. An hour and forty-five minutes to go before he had to meet her at headquarters.

"I'm going to check on the llamas," Rory said, pushing himself back from the table. "You want to come with me?"

"Sure." Anything to get away from discussing his marital status and romantic involvement. Or lack thereof.

"Cleanup on aisle five," Geneva snapped, fanning her cards toward the littered table.

Rory shrugged. "I thought maybe you and Red might want the rest."

"There's not enough left for a dieting mouse," Red grumbled as Rory and Mack quickly cleared and wiped down their end of the table.

As the two stepped outside into the cool night, Mack

could hear Geneva say, "Honey, I made *us* pimento-cheese sandwiches and some banana pudding…"

The spring peepers were giving full voice to their shrill mating song. The scent of woodsmoke drifted through the valley. There wasn't a cloud in the starry sky. The temperature had already dropped dramatically, forecasting a cold and uncomfortable surveillance.

Rory walked across the barnyard to lean on the inner pasture fence. Within seconds a llama appeared out of the darkness. "Hey, Percy. Want some carrot?" He dug into his pocket. "Samantha will be home in two days, and you won't be able to have breakfast with Red in the bunkhouse."

Mack chuckled. The curmudgeonly old farmer had fallen for these strange creatures Garrett's wife had introduced.

"Samantha says we might be getting another llama," Rory said, his voice filled with excitement. "For me. The original six would still be used for trekking, but I could train the new one and enter him in regional competitions."

Rory wanted more than anything to be a country vet. As he talked on about the prospect of caring for his very own llama, Mack thought of how lucky this kid was. With two—now three—loving parents, a safe community, the certainty that he'd go to school, the opportunity to travel.

Unlike the kids Mack had met in Iraq.

"I need to shove off," he said abruptly. "I want to shower before my shift."

"Okay." Rory gave Percy the last of the carrot slices. "I'm gonna make sure the rest of the herd has plenty of hay. It's supposed to get cold tonight. I'm glad the shearer hasn't come yet."

"If I don't see you before, I'll definitely see you at the reception on Sunday."

"You bet!"

Mack poked his head in the kitchen door to say his goodbyes to Geneva and Red, then hit the road. He didn't return to headquarters directly. Although he did want to shower before his shift began, he had plenty of time. He needed to be alone for a bit. Without the inevitability of running into other deputies in the barracks. Or the possibility that Chloe would show up early. Even hanging out with Rory, Red and Geneva—old friends—was painful after a while.

Sometimes he felt like a fraud.

He left the county two-lane to follow a logging road that ended at an abandoned quarry. He shut off the engine to gaze out over the water-filled pit with its reflection of stars and the rising moon. After he'd returned from Iraq, for the six months he'd lost himself in alcohol, he'd tramped this county on foot. Now he couldn't go anywhere that wasn't tainted by dark memories.

Samantha had finally dragged him to AA. Red had put him up in the bunkhouse. Garrett had saved his job for him in the department, then urged him to move into the barracks. And now that he was back on the force, now that he was off the booze and could look a person in the eye and carry on a conversation, everyone thought the old Mack was back.

But the old Mack was dead.

And no one had stepped in to fill the void.

Dammit. His sponsor had warned him to avoid being alone as much as possible. Not to go over and over old territory. That was a slippery slope toward the first drink.

He turned the key in the cruiser's ignition. Hell, there were real bad guys to be collared. Much easier than fighting ghosts.

DRESSED IN LAYERS OF WARM clothing, Chloe sat in the small, downstairs waiting area. She didn't know what to expect tonight. Not after Mack had turned the tables on her this morning.

She'd spent the day regaining her balance. After attending Hannah Breckinridge's fire-safety talk at the seniors' center, Chloe had made a point of interviewing all the deputies in depth. Maybe concentrating on Mack had been a mistake.

"Ready to go?" Mack stood over her, dressed in sweats and carrying a large thermos. It was the first time she'd seen him out of uniform. His hair was damp and he smelled of soap, but he needed a shave and looked more than a bit dangerous.

"G-great minds think alike," she stammered, holding up her own thermos. *Weak, Chloe,* she thought. *Really weak.*

As she bent to pick up her backpack, he put his hand on her shoulder. "Not tonight. This is an ongoing investigation. You're not to take photos or write about specifics. You can write about procedure and your impressions *after* the fact, but nothing that might identify this operation."

"I understand."

He took what was essentially her toolbox and stowed it next to the night dispatcher behind the front desk. Now she felt exposed.

She followed him down Main Street to an old, beatup truck parked in front of the drugstore. "Hop in," he said.

She was immediately disconcerted by the closeness of the cab and the bench seats. And retrofitted seat belts. And a gearshift on the steering column. "How old is this thing?"

"I learned to drive on it," he said. "When I was in middle school."

"You drove when you were in middle school?"

"Hey, the sheriff was with me."

"But you're the same age."

"Welcome to rural America. I think my father might have learned to drive on it, too."

As Chloe digested that personal tidbit, they drove to the county fairgrounds outside town where hundreds of cars were parked around several exhibition buildings. It seemed the entire population of Colum County had shown up here tonight.

"Livestock auction," Mack said, stopping next to the largest building. "It should be winding down in a couple hours. The character we're looking for is supposed to be making the rounds here."

"What's the name?"

"You don't need to know that. We're only on lookout tonight. He's sure to make connections. We'll pick up his trail and see where he goes and who he sees. It's so early in the investigation, we may run into a dead end."

Chloe followed Mack into a brightly lit exhibition hall that smelled of cigarette smoke and animals. There were cattle, horses, sheep, pigs, goats, donkeys, llamas and poultry for sale. While an auctioneer held forth in a central ring, people milled about the livestock pens on the periphery. Mack guided her to a crowded section of the bleachers, presumably so they wouldn't draw attention to themselves. Although Chloe couldn't fathom how a deputy sheriff—a local boy, to boot—could expect to have much luck as an undercover agent. Not here.

But Mack wasn't acting particularly secretive.

"Who or what are we looking for?" she whispered once they'd sat down.

He ignored her, a sure signal to be silent. Her bad.

For all she knew, the perp could be sitting right behind them.

"That's a fine-looking cow," she said in her sweetest voice, pointing to a great lummox being led into the ring. "Can we buy it, dear? I get so tired of running to the store for milk."

Someone in a seat ahead of them sniggered.

"If you get milk out of that *steer,* darlin'," Mack drawled, putting his arm around her and pulling her tightly against his side, "you'd better call the *Guinness Book of World Records.* Now hush."

Sadly he released her. Against all reason, she liked being close to him. Liked the almost circus atmosphere of the auction. Liked pretending they were a couple. That was an admission that didn't need to make it to print.

Mack put his mouth to her ear. "Across the ring," he whispered, his breath hot. "Keep your eye on the guy with the John Deere cap and the Tar Heels sweatshirt."

She saw him. He didn't look like a farmer. With his hat on backward, he looked like a college kid. A computer geek, even. Who worked the crowd like a politician. From their seats in the bleachers, they could easily monitor his movements without attracting notice. Throughout the proceedings, people snapped photos of livestock on their cell phones and text-messaged furiously before making bids. Mack took several pictures of the guy in the green cap.

Around 1:00 a.m., when the auction was winding

down—and she could no longer feel her backside—
the subject hooked up with another man and headed
for the exit. Pretending he was interested in a hog
penned near the two, Mack snapped a quick photo.

"Let's get some air," he said, rising and stretch-
ing. At the exit he leaned against the wide door frame
and pulled her close to him again. "Pretend you're
gazing at the stars," he instructed, his voice low and
far too sexy.

It wasn't hard to get lost in the ruse. The night was
cold and crystal clear. Mack's embrace was warm
and strangely comforting. She'd always been a
woman to take care of herself, but if she needed to
pretend, she could take a few minutes to lean on this
strong man.

All too quickly, Mack urged her toward his pickup.
Apparently *he* hadn't gotten lost in the make-believe.
Had actually been paying attention to business.

He revved the engine and turned the heater up, but
didn't leave the parking lot.

"What are we waiting for?" she asked.

"Country surveillance is more difficult than city
surveillance. There's not much traffic to blend into.
We have to be cautious."

"Don't they know you already?"

"Not personally. The guy in the John Deere
cap's from Charlotte. We don't have a sheet on the
other one."

"What's John Deere driving?"

"Over there." Mack pointed through the windshield to a muscle car covered with primer and stripped of its chrome. "The Camaro."

"That doesn't look any better than your truck or my Yugo."

Mack grunted. "Believe me. A ton of custom work's already been poured into that baby. And there he goes. The other guy's with him." He put the pickup in gear.

"How are we ever going to keep up with him?"

"Don't let appearances fool you," he said as he stepped on the accelerator and spun out of the parking lot in a shower of pebbles. "There's custom work under this old hood, too."

"Omigod!" she exclaimed as she slid across the bench seat and into him. "You don't have to drive like a lunatic!"

"Buckle up."

As the car in the distance slowed for a curve, Mack slowed the pickup, as well, giving Chloe time to wrestle with her seat belt.

"Won't he know we're following him?" she asked.

"That depends on how far we have to tail him. There aren't many places you can go around here at this hour, except home. The kids sometimes drag race out by the old airstrip, but we run a regular patrol out there to break things up. I don't suppose this guy would want to conduct a meeting where the sheriff's department is known to show up at any time."

Mack expertly maneuvered a series of hairpin turns as Chloe slid back and forth on the hard plastic seat despite being buckled up. With all the jouncing, she was going to need a bathroom soon.

"Of course, there are a couple 'private clubs' back in the hollows. If he heads for one of those, we're going to be reduced to pulling into the bushes or driving back and forth until the Camaro's on the move again."

He slowed as their headlights picked up a deer with her fawn standing like lawn ornaments by the roadside.

"Then there's Phil's Eats, a twenty-four-hour joint over the county line."

"Have you considered he might call it a night and go home to bed?" she asked.

"Not him. He thinks of himself as a real player. A not-so-big fish in a small pond is what he is. But it's his overblown ego that's going to eventually do him in."

Despite Mack's boast that the truck had considerable custom work under the hood, the heater wasn't cranking out much warmth. Chloe pulled the cuffs of her sweatshirt over her fists. "What are you hoping to accomplish tonight?"

"At this point we just want to observe his contacts. And Phil's Eats it is," he declared as the Camaro made a right under a neon sign up ahead.

Mack pulled over to the side of the road and waited a full five minutes, letting a half-dozen cars enter and exit the diner's parking lot before pulling in himself. Through the big plate-glass windows, Chloe could see that the two men from the auction were seated in a booth and were now joined by a third man.

"The plot thickens," she said as Mack found a spot in the crowded lot. "Do you know the new guy?"

"Sort of." Mack backed into a position that afforded an indirect view of the front door. "Enough that I wouldn't feel comfortable showing myself inside."

"Don't yell at me, but I have to pee," Chloe admitted when he finally came to a stop.

He sighed, then pulled a twenty from his pocket and handed it to her. "You go in. Order us some takeout. Anything. While you wait, use the bathroom."

"What if they decide to leave before—"

"Don't worry about that. Now go."

She went into the diner and ordered burgers, fries and a couple of sodas to go, then used the restroom. The three men were still there, huddled in heated discussion, when she came out and paid, and still there when she headed for the pickup.

Back in the cab she and Mack ate in silence, while he fixated on the scene inside the diner—the men drinking cup after cup of coffee and talking, talking, talking. Because Mack didn't acknowledge her presence, she gathered their trash and was about to get out to throw it in the bin by the door when the three men stood up, paid and stepped out into the parking lot.

"What if the guy you *sort of* know recognizes you?" she asked, her heart racing at the thought of discovery.

Mack didn't answer. Instead, he pulled her to him and kissed her hard. So hard she found it difficult to breathe. When she finally came up for air, she tried unsuccessfully to phrase a question. "What—?"

"Be quiet." His lips hovered above hers. "For all they know, we're a couple of kids making out."

Okay. She could do this.

Especially since he did it so well.

She wondered briefly where and with whom he practiced, before surrendering to the second kiss. Or was it the third? Or maybe the fourth? Whatever. She threaded her fingers through his hair and heard him groan. Was that part of the act?

She didn't care.

This was *soooo* inappropriate.

She didn't care.

He felt and smelled and tasted too good. And she must not have felt half-bad, either, because his hand was under her jacket, under her layers of clothing, on her bare skin.

He sucked in air, pulled back. "You don't wear a bra?"

"No," she said between gasps. "Do you?"

The Camaro pulled out of the parking lot, three men now inside.

"Buckle up," Mack ordered for the second time

tonight, his hands returning to the wheel. How could that be? She still felt them on her skin. Still felt the rush of his kiss. But he sat erect, staring through the windshield, in full control of, not only his hands, but his emotions. Apparently hot kisses were a routine part of surveillance. No biggie.

For him.

She'd need *a lot* more practice before she ever regarded them as ho-hum.

CHAPTER TEN

MACK DIDN'T KNOW WHAT riled him more: that this surveillance, with a reporter tagging along, had the potential to become more than boring routine; or that he'd gotten lost in the diversionary kiss with said reporter.

He was careful not to follow the Camaro too closely. His pickup looked like a hundred other farm trucks in the area. If the subject had noted its presence at both the auction and the diner, no big deal. But a third time heading in the same direction? Cause for suspicion, if the guy had a brain in his head.

When the Camaro turned to cross Duffy's Creek, Mack had a good idea he'd be heading for the "private club" in Watkins Hollow.

"Why aren't you following?" Chloe asked as Mack drove past the turn off.

"I know where he's going. But I don't want him to think we're going there, too."

Mack drove a mile farther, then did a tire-squealing, two-point turn in the road before heading back toward the creek crossing. A couple of miles past the bridge, he shut off his headlights then came to a stop within sight of the Watkins property and a large vegetable stand. It was there that Ione Watkins sold produce by day and Owen Watkins entertained his cronies by night. Up until now the nighttime get-togethers hadn't been serious enough to warrant the sheriff's interference. They involved some drinking. Some cards. A lot of BS. A congenial spot to float the idea of a fake-lottery-ticket scam.

Several cars and trucks, including the Camaro, were parked in front of the stand. The building's rough shutters were closed, but light leaked out around the edges and smoke trickled out of the chimney. Downwind and on the other side of the road, Mack backed the pickup deep into the under-brush, but not so deep he couldn't keep an eye on the activity up the road. Anyone driving by would simply think the old truck was abandoned.

"You're not going to have any paint left," Chloe protested as branches clawed at the fenders.

"That's the beauty of a farm truck like this," he replied, shutting off the engine. "It's seen worse. Besides, it's what's under the hood that counts."

"What now?" she asked as a country quiet descended on them.

Exactly. What now? Mack couldn't help but think of the wait ahead—maybe hours. Alone with Chloe.

"Coffee," he said, and reached for his thermos. "That's next."

She reached for hers, as well, then immediately put it back on the floor.

"It's going to be a long night," he cautioned. "If you want to get a good notion of surveillance, you're going to have to stay awake."

"I know. But if I drink all this coffee, at one point I'm going to have to...you know."

He indicated the great outdoors surrounding them. "Pick your spot."

She looked dubiously out her window.

"Did you ever hear the story," he said, "of the escaped convict with the hook—"

"Don't!" She swung her arm and belted him across the chest. Luckily he hadn't unscrewed the top to his coffee. The thermos clattered to the floor. "How did the sheriff choose to leave an adolescent in charge? He might as well have deputized his son."

"Well, we're going to have to talk about *something* until dawn."

"Turn the radio on, then."

"The battery would be dead in no time. Hey, Darden warned you surveillance is mostly boredom."

"And cold," she griped. The warmth from the heater was quickly escaping the cab.

"Come on. Toughen up, Atherton. You're wearing long underwear."

Her sharp intake of breath told him she remembered how he knew. When he'd slipped his hand under her clothes while they were kissing. When he'd discovered she wasn't wearing a bra. It might be pitch-black in the truck, but his wandering thoughts were in cinematic color.

"I can take you back to town," he offered. "These guys will more than likely be here when I return."

"You'd like to get rid of me, I'm sure."

"Not true," he admitted—albeit reluctantly—and was glad he'd insisted she leave her tape recorder behind.

When she had no retort, they lapsed into an awkward silence. He poured himself a cup of coffee and drank it staring out the window at the vegetable stand. The woman was a thorn in his side. He actually did want her gone—at the same time he wanted her pressed up against him.

"About this morning," he said at last. Better to talk about that gaffe than the kiss. "I didn't mean to hurt you by looking up your name. I only wanted to make a point."

This time she didn't shrink from him. "You asked me why, in light of my family's tragedy, I became a reporter."

"I said you don't have to answer that."

"I need to." She took a deep breath.

He waited.

"When it looked as if I might be clinically depressed," she said slowly, "despite family counseling, despite individual counseling, my mother—a scientist and very analytical—took matters into her own hands."

Chloe picked up a napkin left over from their takeout and began to shred it. Mack wanted to stop her, but that would involve touching. Too intimate. Too dangerous.

"I don't know how Mom did it," she continued. "She had her own grief to bear. But she started me on a course of facing reality. Oh, she didn't call it that. She merely steered me away from the fiction section when we visited the library. Toward nonfiction. She monitored my TV viewing and my movies. We saw a lot of IMAX documentaries at the natural-history museum."

The napkin shredded, she started on the takeout bag. He felt helpless to stop her.

"Her mantra became 'The truth stays independent of hurt or help.'"

"Harsh." He thought of Nate. Of Tanya.

"No. It's unemotional reality. Truth just *is*. My mother believed if she could teach me to face up to that, I'd survive. Claire was dead. I hadn't meant for her to die. My parents had to get beyond what-if to survive. So they concentrated on their love for each other. Their love for me. Work. The world at large that went on despite our grief."

Cold. He shivered at their dispassionate approach to tragedy—until he thought of his own. Descent into alcohol. "Recovery" at a price—pushing everyone away.

"That's why I became a reporter," she said. "I stick to the facts and try to get close to the truth."

"Are you really that tough?" He meant it as a compliment.

"No one's as tough as they make out," she shot back, scooping up the shredded paper and stuffing it into what remained of the takeout bag. "Not even you."

"And what gives you that idea?"

"When I talked to Tanya Donahue—"

"You're not going to write about Tanya."

"Why not? Her position is deplorable. People need to read how vets' families are faring. And your attempt to help her is admirable. The public also deserves to know how you go above and beyond your duties as a deputy."

Now he was getting pissed off. Exposure was another form of touch. "This friggin' article isn't about me."

"Actually, my editor's considering making it into a series."

"There's not enough story for a brief scroll across the bottom of the screen on the local news channel." He glanced at the vegetable stand. No more vehicles had arrived. None had left.

"Let us be the judge of that," she said.

"You are so naive," he said, turning to her. "You have no idea what's a story and what's not. What constitutes facts, even. Weren't you the one who initially thought I was accepting a bribe from Burt and buying drugs from Duke?"

"Yes. And at first I thought Tanya was a hooker."

He slammed the steering wheel with the flat of his hand. "Why would you think that?"

"I'm sorry, but I followed you the first night I was—"

"That's it. I'm taking you back to June's."

Before he could act, she pulled the key out of the ignition, then rolled down her window and dangled the ring outside.

"Don't you dare," he growled, coiled to lunge.

"I'll make a deal," she said. "One key in exchange for an honest conversation."

He drew back against his door. "About what?"

"Tell me what makes a lawman tick."

He tried to think in generalities. "Most of us aren't sinners or saints."

He held out his hand, and she dropped the keys into it.

Cranking up the window, she said, "Then let me pick your brain. Getting the facts isn't a single answer. Or a one-shot interview. It's a process."

So was getting rabies shots.

"What makes Deputy Whittaker tick?" Chloe persisted. Since he'd returned home, no one had pressed him as this woman had. Pressed him to confront things better left buried. "I want to know about the hometown sports star, the law officer and the war vet."

At *war vet* he pulled the hood of his sweatshirt over his head. Crossed his arms over his chest in an attempt to warm himself. It didn't work. "The truth isn't always neat and tidy and reportable."

"I'm aware of that," she replied, her voice no longer challenging. He didn't know if he could accept her understanding.

"And it's not necessarily good," he continued. "More often than not, it's raw and ugly and inexplicable."

"I can handle it."

Yeah? Well, maybe this was the way to exorcise his demons. Maybe if she knew what he'd done and showed the disgust he was certain she'd feel, then left town, taking the sorry mess with her, he could face the people who remained. Maybe it wasn't Tanya who was supposed to help him begin his penance. Maybe it was Chloe.

"The army part is off the record," he insisted.

She paused. "Okay."

"The *truth,*" he said, seriously doubting he'd have the stomach to finish the story, "is going to Iraq with the 'noble' aim of helping a people…and then finding the world turned upside down."

She didn't say a word.

"When I deployed, I was like a thousand others. I knew troops got killed. But *I* wouldn't. I had too much to live for. I had a job. I had a girlfriend. I wanted a family. I loved kids. Over there…I saw kids in unimaginable situations."

She inhaled sharply but didn't speak. A car passed

on the road, briefly illuminating her face. Her eyes were as wide as those of the doe they'd caught in the headlights a while back. He bet she already questioned what kind of man he'd prove to be.

"Now Nate, he had kids of his own," he continued, strangely unable to stop himself. "Loved them fiercely. But over there, he shut down where the Iraqi kids were concerned. It was as if he didn't see them. Didn't want to understand their situation."

"Maybe," she said softly, "when you have children of your own, you see your child in every other. It could tear your heart out. Maybe shutting down was Nate's only defense."

"Or maybe he was smarter than me."

"How so?"

"I began befriending some of the kids. Giving them gum. Candy. Sometimes rations. Many of them were so malnourished you couldn't tell their age." He ran his fingers around the steering wheel. Its cold, smooth surface an anchor to the present. "Nate warned me to remain detached."

"But you didn't."

"No." He didn't want to go on, but felt compelled to. "There was one boy in particular. A street orphan, so willing to please. He reminded me of Rory. Although he was probably older. I began letting him run simple errands. Gave him some money. Not much. The guys couldn't pronounce his name, so they called him Joe. He acted as if he took pride in the nickname. It was like he was the unit mascot. To everyone except Nate."

"Nate didn't trust the kid."

"Not at all. But Nate didn't trust anyone over there. I thought he'd lost his soul. Instead—"

At the vegetable stand, someone came out. Mack sat up. He grabbed the night binoculars from the floor. But the guy merely pulled a carton of cigarettes out of his car, then went back inside.

"Go on," Chloe quietly urged.

"I didn't see what happened that day. I was getting ready to take a shower. All I know is from hearsay and the investigative report…and looking at the bomb site." He faltered.

"Tanya said it was a suicide attack…"

"Yeah." Despite the chill in the cab, sweat beaded his forehead. He could hear the noise of the explosion. The shouts. As if they were happening around him now. "A kid with a homemade bomb strapped to his chest."

"Joe?"

"So it…appeared. Apparently, another faction was recruiting with something more powerful than gum and candy." He found himself shaking uncontrollably. "The way I see it…*I*…fragged my own buddies."

Struggling to breathe, Chloe sat in her corner of the truck. She understood one thing—Mack lived with the feeling that there were no calculable number of good deeds he could do to atone for this one day in his past.

She understood.

"It was a mistake of horrific proportions," she said at last. "But it was a mistake."

"Don't try to whitewash it," he replied tonelessly.

Without thinking, she leaned across the cab and kissed him gently on the lips.

He pulled away. "Do all women think pity and a kiss can take care of everything?"

Her head snapped back as if he'd slapped her. "No." She looked out her window at the thick underbrush and fought back tears. "They only make you feel alive," she added on a whisper.

He grabbed her with an alarming ferocity. Kissed her as if trying to prove something. To her or to himself, she couldn't know.

From the minute she'd seen Mack en route to Applegate that day, she'd been attracted to him. Had tried not to ask what it would be like to let herself want him.

Well, now she knew.

She let herself respond to his rough kisses. To his demanding touch. Shoving the hood away from his head, she straddled his lap, kissed and nipped and licked his face, his ears, his neck. He rubbed his unshaven jaw against her skin and made her shudder. Laid her back against the bench seat and tugged at her jeans.

"No!" She pushed him away. "I can't!"

"Dammit!" Breathing heavily, he loomed above her.

She wriggled out from under him and pushed herself against the passenger door. "*We* can't."

Slowly he sat back on his side of the seat. "Of course not," he ground out. She couldn't tell if he was angry at her or himself or both. But he was angry, no doubt about it.

"We're working together," she said. That wasn't the reason, but she'd rather he believed the lie. In truth, she couldn't make love to him because they'd forged a real connection. An emotional connection. One she'd never let herself feel with any other lover. Sex with him now would land her in unmarked and dangerous territory.

"We have to get out of here," he said harshly.

"What about the Camaro? What about the surveillance operation?" *What about us?* she wanted to ask. *What have we done?*

"We know who the lead guy is. We now have two contacts. The next shift will pick up the trail." He pulled her roughly back to the driver's side as he opened the door and stepped out. "Do you know how to jump a vehicle?"

"I've had to do it with my Yugo too many times to count. But why—"

"I don't want anyone to hear the truck's engine start."

"You're going to push us out of this underbrush?" This wasn't like rolling her Yugo down the apartment driveway in Brevard.

"We're on a slope. It shouldn't be too hard."

Not as hard as staying in the cab and confronting what had happened between them.

"Give me some direction," she said.

"When I get you onto the pavement, turn right. The road runs downhill to the creek bridge. You should be able to pick up speed easily. Keep the clutch in, and don't let it out till you get past the first turn, then start her. You'll be out of sight by then."

"And where will you be?"

"Running right behind you. Now release the emergency brake and put it in Neutral. And don't put your lights on till the engine's running." He closed the door carefully. The click was almost inaudible.

As she settled behind the wheel, glad for *something* to do, he began to rock the truck.

On the fifth lurch forward, the pickup began to roll. She turned her head to the left to make sure no car was coming, then turned the truck right onto the pavement. It was dark under the trees and hard to see more than a few yards ahead. It would be next to impossible for an oncoming car to see her. Before it was too late.

The road sloped more steeply than she remembered, and too quickly for comfort she picked up speed. The only sound was the hiss of tires on damp pavement and the pounding in her ears. In the rearview mirror she saw a shadowy figure running behind her. She could only hope it was Mack.

The curve came up much too soon and she

swerved on a frost-slicked patch, nearly running into the opposite ditch. As she righted the pickup, she popped the clutch. The engine came to life, then settled into a purr as she hit the brakes.

Shortly afterward, the driver's door opened and Mack shoved her over to slide behind the wheel. He hit the accelerator, and they clattered over Duffy's Creek bridge.

He didn't say another word to her. Not even when he dropped her off in front of June's bed-and-breakfast.

CHAPTER ELEVEN

IN HER ENTIRE LIFE HAD she ever done anything more reckless?

As the first rays of sun touched June's garden, Chloe stood in the cold on the sidewalk, watching Mack drive away. June had covered her flower beds with sheeting to protect them from the frost that now blanketed the lawn. Chloe wished she could pull a protective layer of something, anything, over herself to hide her past mistakes from the rest of the world. From Mack.

Chloe Miranda Atherton, what were you thinking? she asked herself as pointedly as she might a difficult interviewee.

She'd spilled her guts to a near stranger. And then she'd almost had unprotected sex with him. Not just anyone, but the subject of a story. And not any story. The one that was supposed to highlight how mature and capable and *professional* she was.

Ha!

Up until now she'd always thought of herself as

a woman who, in her life and in her work, recognized consequences.

Mack, too, had to have been thinking about how inappropriate the whole situation was, or he'd have said *something* to her on the ride home.

She dragged herself into the B and B, and, avoiding the kitchen, where June would be baking for breakfast, headed up to her room for a long, restorative soak in the tub, then, hopefully, sleep. The bath was easy. Sleep was not. She tossed on the big four-poster bed and thought of Mack. His big heart. His flawed judgment. His confession.

And of his body and how he had seemed as ready as her to throw consequences to the wind.

Chloe knew that Mack couldn't care for someone until he forgave himself. But could he do that?

How had she come to care so much in five days?

Pulling the pillow over her head, she slept fitfully until the sound of a delivery truck woke her. It was ten-fifteen. Saturday morning.

With less than three hours' sleep, she was wide-awake. She had to talk to Mack.

After hastily dressing, she avoided June once again on her descent through the house. She didn't need a perceptive woman trying to read her feelings right now. Because even *she* didn't know what her feelings were.

Walking the few blocks down Main Street to the sheriff's office, she saw that the sun had completely melted the frost. A week ago this town had merely been a location for an assignment. Now…she'd miss the place when she left.

Inside, behind the call desk, Hannah Breckinridge twisted her long blond hair into a braid, then a coiled knot that would fit under her Stetson. "This yours?" she asked, lifting Chloe's backpack above the counter.

"Thanks." Chloe grasped the straps of her mobile office, glad of an apparent excuse for her morning visit—when she'd be expected to be in bed, catching up on her post-surveillance sleep.

"How'd it go last night?" the deputy asked.

"It…was cold." And hot, hot, hot.

"Yeah. Mack's got a ways to go when it comes to personal relationships." Hannah rolled her eyes. "And the weather was supposed to be nippy, too."

Chloe smiled weakly. "Is he in? But then, he's probably sleeping."

"No. He checked in, then left. Earlier in the week he mentioned something about Pete and Emma Donahue having their first soccer game today."

"Where would that be?" Chloe cleared her throat and pretended to search through her backpack. "I need to…go over a few things before I begin writing up my final copy."

Hannah eyed her as she might a lying suspect. "The municipal ball fields. Out about a mile and a half on the road to Asheville."

"Thanks, Hannah," Chloe said, trying for breezy. "Later."

"At the Pillar and Post tonight?"

She'd forgotten all about that. "I don't know," she called over her shoulder. "That depends on…how far I get with this story."

With her life, was more like it.

"Come on," Hannah urged as Chloe reached the door. "Don't reporters get to have R & R?"

Rest and relaxation. Rock and roll. Randy and randier. Thinking both she and Mack had experienced too much of the latter, Chloe hurried back up Main Street to her Yugo, then drove to the municipal fields where two teams of Peewee players were already running up and down a soccer pitch in organized chaos. When she pulled into the parking lot, she could see Tanya with Wayans perched on her hip, cheering on Pete and Emma from the sidelines. Mack was nowhere in sight.

"Hey, Tanya," Chloe said, getting out of her car. "Who's winning?"

"Who can tell?" There was color in Tanya's cheeks today, and some sparkle in her eyes. "I wanted to let you know Frank Hudson called. He's going to let me stay in the house. We worked out a reduction in rent based on the repairs Mack did, and ones I promised to do in the future. He called it the 'GI Package.' I'll still have to get a job, but my sister will help with the kids, and Mack helped me figure out a budget."

"That's terrific. Although instead of the 'GI Package,' I think I'd call it the 'Mack-Convinces-Frank Package.'"

"Mack? I thought it was the threat of press coverage that did it. You."

Chloe blushed at the thought she might have had something to do with Frank's turnaround. "Whatever. I'm just glad you won't have to disrupt your home."

"You and me both," Tanya said as Wayans began making goo-goo eyes at Chloe.

"B-by the way…" It had been a very long time since she'd put herself in contact with children. "Deputy Breckinridge said I might find Mack here."

"I haven't seen him," Tanya replied, nuzzling her son's neck. "He registered Pete and Emma in the soccer league, and he said he'd try to attend their first game. But with all he has to do in the aftermath of the storm, I don't know where he could be."

"He worked the eleven-to-seven shift and went right back out. Does the man ever sleep?"

"The deputies say no." A look of motherly concern suffused Tanya's features. "Boy, he must be beat. So don't give him a hard time about the kids' game when you do catch up with him. There'll be others. But do tell him our electricity finally came back on. One less thing for him to worry about."

At that moment Wayans reached his pudgy arms out to Chloe. Startled, she asked, "What does he want?"

"Why, he wants a hug." Tanya stepped closer. "He's my cuddle-bug. Spreads love wherever he goes."

Clasping her hands behind her back, Chloe tried not to look horrified. "I—I'm sorry. I'm not very good with children."

Tanya's eyes opened wide. "That's not what Wayans thinks. But we won't push. Will we, cuddle-bug?" She gently tickled him until he turned his full attention back to her.

"I guess I'll…see you around," Chloe said, backing away.

"I hope so." Tanya regarded her intently. "If I didn't tell you before, don't be a stranger after your assignment here is finished."

"I'll try not to be." She'd been thinking she might ask her editor if she could do a series on military families. But that would involve getting close to— duh—families. How could she do that if she couldn't even hold a toddler?

With a nervous wave in Wayans's direction, Chloe escaped to the Yugo, where she tried to focus. Think of other places she might find Mack. It troubled her that she didn't know him well enough to know his haunts. Whistling Meadows came to mind. If he wasn't there, his godson might point her in the right direction.

As she drove to the McQuires' farm, she tried to formulate what it was she actually wanted to say to Mack, but all she could think about was Wayans's dimpled hands reaching out to her.

She switched on the radio and searched the dial. She found a static-filled AM station out of Brevard— 1980s country. When the DJ played "Jose Cuervo," Chloe let loose with an off-tune singalong that rattled the dashboard all the way to Whistling Meadows. This kind of letting loose wasn't like her. But it felt good.

As she turned into the private lane, she saw the small herd of llamas cavorting in the field closest to the road. Apparently an overnight hard frost made them frisky. She shivered to think of what she'd almost succumbed to in the bracing chill last night.

Pulling into the barnyard, she saw Rory and Red repairing the paddock gate. "How's it going?" she asked in greeting.

"We're making sure everything's A-okay," Rory replied. "That way Samantha will feel she can leave us in charge anytime."

"And the sheriff will feel he can take some of his accumulated vacation time," Red added. "Can leave Mack in charge until *Mack* finds a reason to take off."

Chloe ignored the invitation to banter. "Speaking of Mack, I'm finishing up my story and have some…issues to clear up. I know he's off duty. Have you seen him?"

"He dropped by earlier to borrow some tools." Sticking his tongue out the side of his mouth, Rory gave the last screw on the paddock-gate hinge a twist.

"Apparently he was going to help his father repair the barn roof today," Red elaborated as he leaned on

the fence and studied Chloe's face. "But when Mack
got to his parents', he discovered that Mel—I believe
you met our mechanic—had organized a crew of
Main Street business owners. A real community
repair bee. I'm not sure Mack appreciated the
surprise. He can give, but has a hard time ta—"

"We're going over as soon as we're finished here,"
Rory interrupted Red with a warning scowl. "You
should check it out for your article."

Yes. A crowd was just what Chloe needed. She
could clear the air with Mack—without risk of
intimacy.

"Hello?" Red stared at her. "I asked if you wanted
to ride with us."

Startled, Chloe shook her head. "No. Thanks. I
need my own car. For mobility."

Rory glanced at the Yugo and chuckled. "If
mobility's what you're after, I'd choose something
other than—"

Red poked the kid in the ribs. "We'll see you
over there."

On the road again Chloe heard a ping, along with
the intermittent rattle and faint grinding noise her
car usually made. Maybe a follow-up visit to Mel
was in order...

No.

She had a perfectly good mechanic in Brevard.
Applegate was nothing more than a temporary assignment.

As the Whittaker farmhouse came in sight, Chloe could see this was no small gathering. Trucks and cars were parked all over the front yard, including a panel truck—a mobile refreshment stand—with "Rachel's Diner" emblazoned on its side. A couple of teenagers set up trestle tables with sawhorses and sheets of plywood while Lily Whittaker, Sarah Culpepper and several other women hurried between the house and the tables with pies, cakes, platters of sandwiches and pitchers of tea. A half-dozen young children were playing tag, it looked like, around a big oak with a tire swing hanging from it. At the barn, volunteers climbed ladders, carried roofing supplies, put down underlay, then shingles, in a well-organized work chain.

Chloe got out of her car and looked for Mack.

"Chloe!" Lily waved with great enthusiasm. "How wonderful you've come!"

Now what? Would she be expected to stay and help?

"Mack!" his mother called. "Chloe's here."

She saw him then. He'd been coordinating the repair effort from the top of the barn, striding back and forth across the roofline with the agility of a mountain goat. The look he shot in Chloe's direction was not one of welcome. He kept working.

Still staring skyward, she stepped forward. Her foot came down on a loose stone, her ankle twisted and she buckled under the pain.

"First the storm, then this," Lily clucked as she rushed to Chloe's side. "Please don't think my home has it in for you," she pleaded, offering her arm for support.

"It's my fault." Chloe waved off her help, but when she tried to take another step, she winced.

"Let's get that ankle elevated and some ice on it right away. No argument now. Lean on me."

Chloe did, and the two women, running a gauntlet of concerned volunteers with plenty of advice, made their way into the house, where Mack's mother helped Chloe recline on the living-room sofa, pillows under her injured leg.

"Thank you, Estelle," Lily said to a very tall woman with stunning silver hair who brought a bag of frozen peas from the kitchen for Chloe to apply to her ankle.

"Lily will have you good as new in no time," Estelle declared. "She has such a way with injured livestock, she should have been a vet."

"Estelle! I do believe you've just called my guest a heifer!"

Chloe chuckled in spite of the persistent pain in her ankle.

"I only meant…" Estelle sputtered to a stop.

"We know what you meant, dear." Lily plumped pillows behind Chloe's back. "Now, bring this lovely young *woman* a glass of sweet tea and a couple of my cheese biscuits."

Red-faced, Estelle returned to the kitchen.

"Please, don't inconvenience yourself for me," Chloe urged, beginning to feel uncomfortable as the object of all this attention. "I'll rest for a minute and then—"

"Heavens, we're just standing in for your mama," Lily replied as she pulled a small table close to Chloe's elbow. "If she were here, she'd be fussing up a storm."

No, she wouldn't. From her home office, she'd ask if there was blood or any protruding bones, then she'd get back to her work with the caveat that Chloe should seek medical attention if ice didn't take care of the pain or swelling.

"Let me see where Estelle is with those refreshments," Lily said, heading for the kitchen.

From the other room Chloe heard Estelle's stage whisper, "Is she the one?"

"Could be," came Lily's breathy reply.

"But that blouse! I had one of those back in the Truman era!"

"Stop it. She's frugal, is all," Lily replied, her voice rising. "An excellent trait. Plus, she has beauty and brains."

"Then go get Mack off that roof. If you want grandbabies anytime in the next century, you need to do some serious matchmaking."

Alarmed, Chloe cleared her throat, and the women in the other room dissolved into shushes and giggles. If she didn't think the cold pack and the elevation were helping her ankle, she'd have scarpered without goodbyes. She took heart in the thought that

Mack would most definitely not come down off the roof to play nursemaid.

The back door slammed.

"Ooh!" Estelle murmured from the kitchen. "Just as if we'd conjured him."

Seconds later Mack stood in the doorway to the living room, glass of iced tea in one hand, plate of biscuits in the other. "Are you okay?"

His hair was rumpled, his chiseled features kissed by the sun and his T-shirt stretched tightly across muscles taut from rigorous physical labor.

"Y-yes." Her pulse ragged, she pushed back into the relative safety of the pillows. "I'm fine."

He strode across the room, placed the biscuits on the table by her side, then handed her the tea and two tablets.

"What are these?" she asked, eyeing them.

"Ibuprofen. Take them or I'm calling the surrogate mothers back in."

Dutifully she washed the pills down with the oh-so-sweet tea, which she almost spilled when, as if he had every right, he lifted the bag of frozen peas to examine her ankle.

"Oh, I bet you're an expert on the care and feeding of livestock, too," she muttered.

He gave her the most curious look. "What are you doing here?" he asked, his tone brusque.

Chloe averted her eyes. "I needed to talk to you about last night, but you're busy."

He looked over his shoulder toward the kitchen, which now seemed unnaturally quiet. After a pause, he pulled up a straight-back chair and sat down. "There are enough people out there that they won't miss me."

Chloe looked down at her hands. Through the open window, she heard a mockingbird's song along with the rat-a-tat of roofing hammers.

He waited.

Sure. Make her do all the work. Stubbornly she set her jaw.

Mack could sense Chloe's whole body tense. He knew her trepidation. In the light of day, how did they talk about last night's craziness?

He ran a thumbnail down the side seam of his jeans. Examined a tar stain just above his knee. "Things got out of hand," he said. "As far as I'm concerned, it's between you and me. Off the record. Besides, we're both adults."

"That's the way I feel." She caught his eye, and he didn't see the regret he'd expected, but desire. There was no mistaking it, and it stunned him. Made him want to throw away all the resolutions he'd made this morning. "But..." she said, playing with the condensation on the glass.

"But?"

"We both know it can't happen again! I'm on assignment. You're my subject."

An uncomfortable pressure radiated up the back of his neck. Pinched the place between his eyebrows. She might be talking about nearly having sex, but he was thinking about the sense of vulnerability that came with his having opened up. Something he hadn't even done at his AA meetings. Today he not only kept his own secrets, but hers, as well. The weight threatened to bring on a migraine.

"Of course we can't let it happen again," he agreed.

"Now that we're both on the same page about *that*," she said, lowering her voice even further, "I also wanted to talk to you about what you told me...before—"

"No," he said, leaning forward, elbows on thighs. "My army experience was a one-time discussion. I got it off my chest, but it's not to go into print."

"It won't. But...I'm concerned about you."

"Don't be." The last thing he wanted was her concern.

"I know how difficult it was for you to tell me about Nate. About Joe." The names grated on his nerves. "I could sense the horror. I can even understand your guilt."

"You can't." Why did she persist in picking at the scab?

"I'm not going to argue with you, because there's a bigger issue now."

"I'm sure you're going to tell me what it is." He looked out the window and wished he was back on the barn roof.

"What I can't understand," she said, "is how you choose to live half a life." As he tried to push his chair away from the sofa, she reached out and grasped his arm. "You say you won't let me write about how you've helped Tanya and her family. Probably not about helping the sheriff, or Burt or your parents, either."

He wrested his arm from her.

"Tanya told me you chip in with expenses on the farm," Chloe said.

"I'm an only child. Giving back to my parents isn't news."

"I guess not. But I understand Mel had to surprise you with a repair bee. It looks as if you're using the secrecy of your very generous acts as a shield. A shield that prevents you from giving *and* taking. From forgiving yourself and moving on."

He glared at her. "It's not up to me to forgive."

"You're the only one left. Tanya never blamed—"

"Are you through?"

"No." Fire in her eyes, she sat upright with a jolt, knocking the package of frozen peas to the floor.

"I know you claim to be after the facts," he said before she could go on. "Getting to the truth. But what I think you're doing is poking around in other people's lives so that you don't have to live your own."

She swung her feet to the floor, so that she was knee to knee with him. "How do you figure that?"

"Even the clothes you wear." He pointed to her shirt, which had secondhand store written all over it.

"They're someone else's, not your own. You fidget when you don't have a notepad or a tape recorder or a camera in your hands. You're fidgeting now."

"No." Awkwardly she pushed up from the sofa. "I'm getting ready to leave."

"Why?" He stood, too. "Clearly, we were just getting down to that honesty you love so much."

"Clearly, we're getting personal. And clearly, our personalities are like oil and water."

"No." He said it so softly, she looked him full in the face. "We're too much alike, you and I. And that's why when we get close, we pop apart. Like the same poles on two different magnets."

A glistening of tears in her eyes was her only answer, an answer she quickly dashed away with her hand. He held back from taking her in his arms and comforting her. Having no comfort for himself, what could he offer?

CHAPTER TWELVE

"OH, DEAR, YOU'RE NOT GOING to wear that!" June exclaimed with dismay. The B and B owner had come up to Chloe's room ostensibly to offer fresh towels.

"May I remind you," Chloe replied, surveying the only dress she'd brought to Applegate and trying to keep her voice from quavering, "this is *not* a date."

As planned, Mack and she were going to the Pillar and Post tonight. It was expected of them. Although, after having escaped from his parents' farm with her dignity barely intact, she was determined to keep the evening strictly businesslike.

What had he said? That they were too much alike. Scary, scary thought.

June lay a hand on her shoulder. "Chloe? Are you all right?"

"Y-yes. I was thinking I should make this an early night. I need to write—"

"Nonsense. Young people need fun." June looked critically at the dress laid out on the bed. "Where did you get that thing?"

"At a great vintage boutique in Brevard."

"I thought so. It will never do. I have slips from Sears sexier than that. I know, I know, it's *not* a date."

Quite frankly Chloe had never paid much attention to her appearance. If she was to be given any attention at all, she wanted it to be for her skills. "What about these?" she asked, pulling her silk trousers from the closet.

"Too Katharine Hepburn. For goodness' sake, she's *my* era. Come on." June dropped the towels on the bed, then dragged Chloe by the hand out of the room and down the hall. Having already been fussed over earlier by Lily Whittaker, Chloe resisted.

"I won't bite," June said as she held tightly to Chloe with one hand and knocked on a guest's door with the other.

A very attractive twenty-something woman answered. With curlers in her hair and a makeup kit in her hand, she appeared to be getting ready to go out, too.

"Chloe Atherton, meet Faith Jackson," June said. "Faith works as a pharmaceutical rep. She's one of my regular guests when she's in the area. Chloe is a reporter in need of a makeover. You two are about the same size. What's in your closet, Faith?"

Chloe was shocked. "I couldn't possibly—"

"Of course you can," Faith replied, pulling Chloe into her room. "Any friend of June's is a friend of mine. Besides, if I were home on a Saturday night, my sisters would be raiding my wardrobe."

"Between us, we have five sisters," June chirped.

"I'm betting you have none," Faith added, looking pointedly at Chloe. "Too much resistance to peeking in another woman's closet."

"Y-you're right." At least not a sister who'd lived to raid her closet.

"Poor girl." Faith began to pull clothing from an antique armoire. "So where are you going tonight?"

"The Pillar and Post," June answered for her.

"It's actually part of an assignment for the *Sun*," Chloe explained. "I'm there to observe, so I don't want to stand out."

"It's always been my observation," June said, "that you learn more as a participant."

Ouch.

Faith held up a sassy moss-green skirt, cut on the bias so that it swung provocatively. "What's your assignment?"

"A week in the life of a deputy sheriff."

Faith's eyes met June's. "Mmm-hmm, *that* deputy," the older woman said. "Need I say more?"

Faith smiled. "Well, then…we're going to have to bring out the potent stuff. I wish I had my whole wardrobe here."

"Hold it!" Chloe threw up her hands. "I'm not trying to catch Deputy Whittaker's attention. I'm going with him—*and* several others tonight—to hear Deputy Rollins perform."

"This might work," Faith said, ignoring her and

laying a simple gold top with three-quarter sleeves and a rather daring neckline above the skirt on the bed. She took a skinny jeweled belt and cinched the top, then put a pair of faux leopard flats on the floor underneath the outfit. "You might have to stuff toilet paper in the toes of the shoes, but otherwise how about it?"

"With her coloring," June said, "it will look stunning. Young and fresh."

"Fun, but not trampy."

"Excuse me, ladies," Chloe protested. "I'm right in the room." Within seconds she felt like Cinderella being dressed by the mice for the ball. Off went the clothes she was wearing. On went...ooh, the fabrics did feel lovely against her skin.

"Now makeup," Faith said, holding aloft a small sponge and several brushes and pushing Chloe into a straight-backed chair.

"I don't wear makeup."

"That's why we're only going to give you the lightest bit of foundation to tone down those freckles, some mascara—you have *fabulous* eyes—and a dab of lip gloss." Faith accomplished the application with a few practiced swipes.

"Now may I look?" Chloe was beginning to think her identity had been hijacked.

"Not before the hair," June said, fingering a strand. "What do you think, Faith? Mousse, then some scrunching to bring out the natural curl? Sit still, Chloe."

"I'm not used to all this concern over my appearance."

"Didn't you ever play dress-up with your mother's things?"

"My mother's an epidemiologist at the CDC," Chloe replied as Faith worked a heavenly scented foam into her hair. "Dress-up would mean wearing her lab coat."

"You poor deprived child."

No. Chloe had always considered herself very lucky to have no-nonsense parents. Their logical, unemotional approach to life made her feel safe.

"I think our work is done, June," Faith declared with a self-satisfied smile. She led Chloe to the tall pier mirror. *"Voilà!"*

The woman staring back in the glass was herself. Only much, much better.

"Those shoes have leather soles," Faith said. "Good for dancing."

"I—I wasn't planning on dancing." Chloe stuck out her leg with the bandage wrapped around the ankle. Her ankle was fine. The bandage was a visual excuse not to dance.

"You'll be dancing, trust me." Faith bustled around the room, picking up articles of rejected clothing. "Now, ladies, I have to pull myself together for a rubber-chicken corporate banquet in Asheville. I wish I was going out with y'all instead."

"Thank you." That was the only thing Chloe could

think to say as the mirror's reflection showed her a woman she didn't quite recognize.

"No problem. And good luck. With your story." Faith winked at June as the B and B owner shepherded Chloe back to her room.

"What time is Mack picking you up?"

"He's not. I told him I'd meet him at the Pillar and Post."

"I wouldn't advise that," June said, pulling a cell phone out of her pocket and hitting a speed-dial number. "I'm surprised he didn't tell you—the parking situation is terrible out there. The vacation-home crowd will be in town for the weekend." She held up her hand. "Kim? Is Mack around? He is? Put him on, please." She shook her head as she waited. "Mack? June. Change of plans. Chloe needs a ride to the Pillar and Post. Okay. See you in a minute."

June snapped her cell phone shut. "Lucky I caught him. He was on his way out the door."

Lucky, sure. "Ms. Parker, you're incorrigible." Chloe had to turn away, grab a tissue, pretend to blow her nose because she was quite overcome at the way this community's women had so thoroughly embraced her.

"Incorrigible?" June asked with a laugh. "Why, it's one of my better qualities. And *you* are simply gorgeous."

Chloe felt gorgeous. It was a dangerous feeling.

INCHES FROM A CLEAN getaway. Mack climbed the B and B's front steps and felt uncomfortably like a suitor.

The day had not gone well. Chloe had said some things that had shaken him. Was he holding himself back from moving on? The thought had plagued him.

"Are you going to come in or should I come out?"

He found himself standing on the stoop and staring through the screen door at…Chloe?

In the soft light of the hallway, she was breathtakingly beautiful. In one very sexy outfit. He was unprepared for the pure physical jolt that shot through him.

This whole evening was not a good idea.

"I'll come out," she said, making the decision for him and stepping through the doorway with a new air about her. A new femininity. A disconcerting sensuality.

He was going to have his hands full keeping the guys off her tonight.

Not that it was any of his concern, but she had a job to do. Her story. Tonight Rollins—primarily, hopefully—was that story. Although Chloe wasn't carrying either her notebook or her tape recorder.

"I hope you don't mind riding in the pickup," he said.

She ducked her head almost shyly, and he regretted that she might think he was alluding to last night. "Hey, it runs better than the Yugo," she replied.

He walked her to the truck. Hell, he might as well

open the door for her. One corner of her mouth tilted in amusement.

"What?" he asked, not ready for the answer.

"I was remembering my first day in town. The first hour. You weren't quite so gallant."

"Drop it, Atherton," he muttered as he walked around to the driver's side. Against his better judgment, he'd promised his mother he'd take care of Chloe tonight.

Not that she needed taking care of.

Next to him on the bench seat, she sat with her legs crossed. The skirt she wore showed them off, unlike the granny dress she'd worn the first day or those baggy trousers. Even the bandage around her ankle was provocative. Hinting at a tender spot he knew lay under that self-possession.

What was her game tonight?

"So," he said when they'd passed the outskirts of town and still hadn't broken the awkward silence, "how's the article coming?"

"My mind's running a mile a minute."

"Have you at least figured out your direction?"

"It's evolving," she replied. "Hey, what time is the sheriff's welcome-home party tomorrow?"

"Three."

"So—" she played with the hem of her skirt "—do you get some extra vacation time when he's back?"

"I don't take vacation."

"Some extra sleep time?"

"I don't sleep."

"Me, neither."

As the conversation came to an abrupt halt, he wondered what kept her awake at night. No, he knew. Her sister had to be as daunting as his buddy. Grief saddled with guilt was a toxic combo. Fourteen years, she'd said. He'd only had a year and a half.

Finally, after he'd counted 137 guardrails, the Pillar and Post came into view. A large, converted barn that housed a regular Saturday-night dance band along with local acts, the place was already hopping, the parking lot full to overflowing. Many of the cars sported out-of-state tags. Newcomers. Weekenders. The deputies who were off tonight had promised to arrive early and snag a table. Rollins was set to go on at nine.

Mack helped Chloe out of the car. At the door he paid the cover price for both of them even as she began to protest. Hey, he was Southern. She was dressed up. His mother would kill him if he didn't pay. Inside the door, he pulled Chloe to a stop and tried to locate their table. Her scent—something very light yet exotic, made him shut his eyes and inhale deeply.

"Over there," Chloe said, startling him back to his senses. "I see Hannah and the others."

The band played a line-dance tune, but few people were on the floor. It was his experience that most folks needed a jump start of liquid courage before strutting their stuff. And the night was young. Un-fortunately. He didn't know how long he could take being close to this new Chloe. As they made their way between the tables, he could see Darden, Sooner and Rollins shaking their heads while they forked over several bills to Breckinridge.

"Hey!" She greeted Mack and Chloe with a smirk when they made it to the table. "Whittaker, never let it be said I don't have faith in you."

"What are you talking about?"

Darden, Sooner and Rollins looked guilty.

"*They* didn't think you'd show."

"The Pillar and Post hasn't been your thing for quite some time," Darden said. "It's good to see you here tonight."

Breckinridge introduced her date, and Darden, Sooner and Rollins introduced their wives to Chloe. Everyone scooted over so two more could fit at the table. Mack took one look at the pitchers of beer that had already been ordered. "I'm going to get a pitcher of Cheerwine Cola," he said, then headed for the bar along one wall.

When he did, Breckinridge pulled Chloe and the three wives out on the floor to join the line dancing. Mack couldn't take his eyes off Chloe. Her hair coppery in the flickering light, she was the most vibrant woman in the room. And in clothing that did her body justice, she was hot.

He'd thought the proximity to alcohol was going

to be the problem tonight. It wasn't. The problem was one beautiful woman he had no business getting involved with.

CHLOE HADN'T HAD SO much fun in a long time. Maybe the change in her attitude was the result of Faith's and June's makeover. Or maybe the camaraderie of the deputies' table lifted her spirits. Or the friendly greetings from townspeople she'd met during the week.

Or maybe it was the unmistakable look of appreciation on Mack's face.

Hey, *nothing* was going to happen. But that didn't mean she couldn't let loose and enjoy the moment. Besides, she needed to prove to him she could step out of her journalistic detachment and embrace life.

Despite his frequent sidelong glances, he'd made no moves. She'd line danced with the women and even accepted some slow dances with the guys Faith had promised would ask. So much for the ankle bandage benching her. At times it appeared as if Mack might cut in, but he didn't. That was okay. They'd put the matter of that middle-of-the-night aberration to bed, so to speak, and it was better they both finished the week on a cordial, but detached note.

"So did you get your story?"

Chloe, now standing in the long line to the

women's restroom, turned around to see Mel, the mechanic. "It's Chloe, isn't it?" Mel added.

This must have been the night for transformations. In an off-the shoulder cotton top, kicky denim skirt and red cowboy boots, the self-described grease monkey was scrubbed clean and apparently ready for a good time.

"Mel!" Chloe exclaimed. "How are you? Yes, I have a story and a half. My editor's thinking of expanding it to a series."

"I see you're at the deputies' table. Couples." Mel gave Chloe's outfit the once-over. "Business or pleasure?"

"Omigosh, business," Chloe replied, trying to sound casual, hoping any color in her cheeks would be attributed to the barn's warm interior. And dancing. "Hannah Breckinridge suggested my story wouldn't be complete without observing some downtime. And Deputy Rollins is performing the next set." She looked toward the front of the line. "I hope I get a chance to see it."

"We can only hope Hannah needs to use the restroom. If she sees the backup, she'll commandeer the men's room until this line disappears. Even off duty, a badge has its perks. And she's not afraid to explore them."

Chloe laughed. She could see Hannah performing such a bold but logical maneuver. She was going to miss this crowd. And the potential for real friendship with Hannah.

"How about Whittaker? Did you ever get him to open up?" Mel asked.

The opening up he'd done wasn't for public consumption. For the first time this week, Chloe felt protective. The feeling surprised her.

"He certainly showed me the ropes," she said with exaggerated enthusiasm. "From patrol during the tornado watch to serving processes to rescuing Sarah Culpepper's cat from a tree."

"I'm glad." Mel leaned against the rough wood planking of the barn wall and stared at Chloe with blatant skepticism. "And I'm glad he's here tonight. Mack's good people. He needs to get back into circulation. Begin to trust again."

A bathroom stall opened up, and with a sense of having escaped, Chloe walked toward it. "See you."

"Anytime."

When Chloe made it back to the table, Deputy Rollins was already tuning his acoustic guitar. Everyone at the table had turned their chairs toward the stage, and Chloe found her seat right up against Mack's. The room lights dimmed and the spotlight was Rollins'.

And Mack draped his arm loosely over the back of her chair.

It wasn't a move, she told herself. He was a big man, and of course he'd need to stretch. But with all the rationalization, the warmth of his arm still made it difficult to concentrate on Rollins, who had a good voice and a half-dozen original songs about love and loss and a couple of bad-ass dogs.

When his set ended, their group broke into a roar of applause. Rollins looked pleased.

Suddenly the smoke and the closeness of all these genial people and the realization that in twenty-four hours she was going back to Brevard and her life of studied detachment got to Chloe. Feeling like Cinderella hearing the clock strike midnight, she stood and said, "I need some fresh air."

"Me, too," Hannah agreed. "I'll go with you."

Although Chloe would have preferred being alone, she didn't argue.

As they passed through the big barn door, the person in charge of admission stamped their hands so that they could get back in. Once outside, Chloe took a deep breath. "Have they never heard of no-smoking laws?"

"Hush. This used to be tobacco country, big time. Every farmer had at least a small patch. Old ways die hard."

Chloe walked farther away from the barn in an attempt to distance herself from the party atmosphere. But the parking lot was jam-packed and appeared to be another venue for socializing and showing off new clothes and comparing restored cars. Did these people do nothing but bond and look out for each other?

Inhaling the bracing night air, Chloe kept moving.

The thought of walking back to town crossed her mind.

"What's wrong?" Hannah asked, putting a hand out to stop her.

"I'm getting a headache.

"I have aspirin."

"No, thanks. Sleep's the cure." Chloe hugged herself and gazed up at the canopy of stars. "I guess I'll see if…someone can drive me home."

"You've been good for him this week."

"Good for whom?" Chloe spun around to face Hannah.

"Mack, of course."

"Ha! I haven't seen him when he hasn't had steam coming out of his ears."

Hannah chuckled. "Believe it or not, that's good for Mack. Until you showed up, he was like a robot. Got the job done, but without any emotion. I don't mean to sound like one of the town matchmakers, but I'd like to see you come back after the article runs. I think Mack would, too."

No. He'd said they were destined to push each other apart. Chloe couldn't stop the fat, hot tear from rolling down her cheek.

Concern clouded Hannah's features. "What did I say? I'm sorry if I brought up a touchy subject."

Overwhelmed by the genuine care and consideration heaped on her this week—from June Parker to Lily Whittaker to Faith Jackson to Hannah—

Chloe couldn't speak. She thought of her less-than-effusive relationship with her own mother, and the tears streamed down her cheeks.

"Hold it together," Hannah said, clearly worried that Chloe had lost it. "I'll get Mack to take you right home."

Home was such a loaded word that it—and less than three hours' sleep in the past thirty-six hours—sent Chloe into sobs.

"Come on," Hannah commanded, pulling Chloe back toward the barn. "Let's find your ride."

Hiding her face in her hands, Chloe shook her head violently. She couldn't let the other deputies see her like this.

"M-Mack…" She meant to say he mustn't see her like this, but she choked on all but his name.

"Of course. I'll get him." Hannah grasped Chloe's upper arms. "Don't move."

As Hannah hurried back into the barn, Chloe tried to get control of herself. People in the parking lot were starting to notice. Maybe, if she could begin to act like a sane person, she could ask one of them for a lift to the B and B. She wiped her eyes. She really, really didn't want Mack to see her like this.

Because she was *not* a hysterical woman.

With years of unerring guidance from her parents behind her, she capped the safety valve on her emotions. Just. But the instant she saw the crowd part and Mack rush toward her, she began to sob again.

As if the safety valve had popped and fourteen years' worth of pressurized sentiment gushed out.

CHAPTER THIRTEEN

"DAMMIT, DID SOMEONE TRY something with you?"
Mack wrapped his arm around Chloe's shaking
shoulders and used his body to screen her from
curious bystanders. Hell, she looked so lovely
tonight he wouldn't put it past one of these guys to
make an unwanted pass.

"Did someone hit on you?" he repeated,
concern—and, yeah, jealousy—rising.

"No!" The one word came out a squeak, washed
away in a new onslaught of tears.

The tears, coming so unexpectedly from Chloe,
of all people, nearly did him in. Roughly he cleared
his throat and concentrated on the next logical step.

"Let's get you out of here," he said, steering her
through the crowded parking lot toward his pickup.

"Wh-where to?"

"To the B and B."

"But the others…"

"They'll think you're exhausted," he said, helping
her into the truck, buckling her into her seat belt. He

hoped exhaustion was the explanation. "Shut your eyes. Get some rest."

She didn't. Of course not. When was the last time she did anything he asked or expected?

All the way back to June's, she might as well have been the one driving. While his attention was drawn to her, she stared straight ahead at the road. Although she'd stopped crying, the light from the dashboard made her cheeks glisten with unwiped tears. Exaggerated the dark circles under her eyes.

When he pulled in front of the inn, he left the pickup idling. Although, for a fleeting moment, he wanted to turn the engine off, carry Chloe up to her room and make sure she was safely tucked in bed.

"Are you going to tell me what's wrong?" he asked.

"Come inside," she said.

He couldn't stop his sharp intake of breath.

"To talk, Whittaker," she added with a rueful smile. "Let's see if June will let us have ice cream."

"Sure." Before opening his door, he met her smile with a frown, not wanting her to think he expected anything but ice cream.

Inside they found June, sleeves rolled above her elbows, tidying the kitchen. "How was the Pillar and Post?" she asked enthusiastically.

"Smoky," Chloe replied, coming to a stop in the middle of the room with an expression on her face that said she'd forgotten what she wanted.

"So now you're looking for a drink?" June prodded.

"More like ice cream," Mack said.

"But your kitchen is closed for the night," Chloe added, turning to leave.

"Nonsense!" June bustled toward the enormous sub-zero freezer. A cloud of condensation enveloped her head when she opened the door to examine the choices. "Faith came home and ate caramel praline crunch. Apparently the hospital fund-raising banquet food was inedible. You're left with vanilla, raspberry swirl, rocky road—"

"Rocky road." Chloe chose so quickly and so vehemently that Mack felt certain she wasn't only referring to ice cream.

"You'll be lucky not to have wild dreams with this much sugar in you at this hour," June said, giving Chloe and Mack a knowing look. She plunked two heaping servings of ice cream, two sheets of paper towel and two spoons on the scarred trestle table. "*Bon appétit!*" With a wave and a wink, she turned out all the lights except the night-light over the stove, then left the kitchen. The now softly, almost romantically, lit kitchen.

Not quite meeting his eyes, Chloe handed Mack a spoon, then sat at the table and dipped her own spoon into the ice cream.

"What happened back at the Pillar and Post?" he asked, sitting but resisting the treat.

Chloe licked ice cream off her spoon slowly. Sensuously. Although Mack doubted her conscious aim was seduction, he pushed his chair away from the table. Away from her.

"This week has been an eye-opener for me," she said. "I came to town to write an in-depth article on a department that's vital to the area."

"I hear a *but* coming," he said, hanging an arm over the back of his chair, trying to remain calm—dispassionate. Was she going to accuse him of stonewalling her efforts?

She tackled another large spoonful of ice cream, closed her eyes and sighed deeply before answering. "But as the week's progressed, I've dredged up questions about myself. Doubts even."

Doubts? This woman had been sure of herself from the get-go. He leaned forward. "I'm not following you," he said. "Doubts about your career? Your life?"

She paused, her spoon in midair. The soft light from the stove backlit the curls framing her head, made her seem ethereal. Like the sad and lost "haints" his granny used to weave into her stories.

"All of that," Chloe said, so quietly he almost thought he'd imagined her speaking.

"To deal with…Claire's death," she continued, "I practiced detachment. Today, your mother, just by being motherly, made me think of my mom…and how we've distanced ourselves from each other. Because I felt guilty for depriving her of a daughter. But—" Her voice caught in her throat.

He began to move his hand across the table to hold hers, but she dropped her spoon and crossed her arms tightly as if she were trying to lock herself away. "No. Let me get this out," she said.

He sat back, helpless. An ugly feeling he thought he'd begun to overcome in the past few months.

"I realized," she continued, her words a painful rasp, "that in distancing myself, I was depriving her of a second daughter."

Bam.

He sat bolt upright in his chair as her revelation triggered something in him. He'd done the same thing she had—hadn't he? The whole town had mourned his buddy Nate when he hadn't returned from Iraq. But Mack hadn't really returned, either. Not the Mack his friends and family remembered. The loss couldn't be easy for them.

He pulled his cell phone out of his pocket and placed it on the table between them. "First a self-inventory," he said. "Then amends."

"Sounds like two of twelve steps," she replied, not loosening the grip she had on herself.

"Whatever." He pushed the phone closer to her. "It's supposed to work."

The look in her eyes was clear and piercing. No tears. "Supposed to work? You haven't tried it."

Touché.

As if it were made of kryptonite, Mack picked up the cell and dialed.

"Ma, it's me. Mack," he said when his mother answered. Before she could jump to the conclusion that disaster had struck, he said, "Everything's okay. I'm about to turn in. I just wanted to let you know that we're back from the Pillar and Post, and I kept an eye on Atherton like you wanted."

"Did you have a good time?" Lily asked.

"Yes. I did," he admitted.

"Then sleep well. I love you."

"I—I love you, too," Mack said, then disconnected. Chloe couldn't know how long it had been since he'd told his mother he loved her. The sincere expression of his feelings lifted his spirits.

Before Chloe could question him, he held out the phone. "Your turn."

Chloe felt Mack's gesture as if it were a physical assault. With a start she stood up. Suddenly the kitchen, which had seemed so warm and comforting, closed in on her. She pushed through the back door to the garden and stood in the moonlight, sucking in great gulps of air. When Mack followed her, she made her way to the old oak tree and the swing, deliberately avoiding the wrought-iron bench, which could accommodate two.

Wrapping her arms around the smooth hemp ropes, she sat on the wooden swing seat. She noticed with satisfaction that Mack wasn't chasing her with the phone. Eyes closed, she lifted her feet and let herself float on the night air. Let the chill envelop her and cool her. She didn't know if she could reach out to her parents—her mother, especially—the way Mack had reached out to Lily.

She heard his boots on the gravel path. Felt his warmth behind her. Smelled the faint scent of his soap. He placed his hands over hers on the ropes. Leaned close so that his lips brushed her ear. Made her eyes fly open and the hair stand up on the back of her neck.

"It's all right," he said in a voice at once tough yet reassuring. "You're strong. You'll eventually do what needs doing."

Before she could answer, he pulled the swing back—way back—then held her suspended above the ground. When she thought he might find some way to leave her hanging until she came to her senses, he gave a tremendous push and sent her swooping on an exhilarating arc.

At the familiar tightening of her stomach, she gasped with pleasure, just as Claire had done so many times when Chloe had pushed her on the playground swings. When Mack pushed more forcefully, she could hear her sister shouting, "Higher!" Could hear her laughter.

Claire, only a toddler, had been all about impetuosity and laughter and unconditional love. And that, Chloe suddenly realized, was what she had abandoned. What she had withheld from her parents. Who probably, despite their stoicism, had always needed as much emotional support from her as she had from them.

On the backswing, when Mack pushed her again, she pumped her legs and shouted, "Higher!" At the top of the forward swing, she let go of the ropes and honestly believed she could fly. And she did. For a couple of seconds before she lost both shoes and landed on the soft, cool grass of June's manicured lawn. She held her sides and let the laughter—and the tears—flow freely.

The borrowed outfit would have to be dry-cleaned—and Mack would think she was nuts—but Chloe lay on her back and made angels in the dew. Mack stood above her, his hand extended, his mouth twitching in a lopsided grin that looked as rusty as her laughter felt.

She took his hand and let him pull her to her feet. "Thank you," she said, feeling pounds lighter.

He held on to her and, with his free hand, brushed a leaf from her hair. Even after the leaf floated to the ground, the sensation of his touch lingered. Excited her. Warned her to be careful. Sharing their secrets was much more intimacy than she'd ever intended.

When he leaned in to kiss her, she pressed the flat of her hand to the middle of his chest. Immediately he released her and stepped back.

"Are you going to be all right?" he asked, his voice brusque as shadows played over his features.

"Yes." It might be the truth *if* she could take the last few minutes and bottle them.

"Then I'll see you one more time tomorrow," he said.

The sheriff's welcome-home party. "Three o'clock. I'll be there." What else was there to say?

Unless she could find a way to maintain her break with the past and live in the present, she couldn't offer up a future.

When he walked out of the garden and around the side of the house, she allowed herself one long, last, moonlit look and felt the bottle of magic minutes break.

She was going to miss Mack.

MACK LOOKED AT HIS watch. Three o'clock on the dot. He'd planned to arrive at the reception before Garrett and Samantha, welcome them with the rest of the community, then duck out at the first opportunity with the excuse of relieving the few members of the staff manning headquarters this afternoon.

Inside the fire hall, people had already arrived by the dozens. June and Rachel had their volunteers, his mother included, lined up to protect the refreshment table. No one, absolutely no one, was getting through that formidable defense until Garrett and Samantha arrived to take the first bite. Chloe had been so busy snapping photos of the preparations, it had been easy to avoid her.

He didn't do goodbyes.

"They're coming!" someone shouted.

The crowd parted to let Garrett and Samantha through, along with Rory, who bounced joyously from one to the other like a golden retriever pup. Sam, of course, was as beautiful and poised as ever. But Garrett—what a change. For a workaholic, the man looked relaxed and happy out of uniform. There must be something to married life—for some people—Mack thought.

He was pleased to see that Chloe didn't force an interview. She took photos, yes, but discreetly. She did follow the family, however, and as they made their way around the hall, Mack knew a meeting— with all four—was inevitable.

Hey, today wasn't about him. Or about a woman so beautiful by moonlight she made him dream what it might feel like to be free to pursue her.

He pasted what he hoped was a smile on his face as Garrett and Samantha drew near. Rory had been sidetracked by the refreshment table, but Chloe stood tenaciously off to the side, her camera ready.

"Congratulations!" he said and meant it as Garrett clapped him on the back.

"It's wonderful to be home!" Samantha planted a kiss on each of his cheeks.

Click. No mistaking that damned camera.

"How was the honeymoon?" Mack asked, turning so that Chloe's lens would be not on him, but on the newlyweds.

"Nothing short of awesome." A look of absolute contentment on his face, Garrett slipped his arm around Samantha's waist, and she nestled against him.

"He ate so much beef and Yorkshire pudding," she said, "I made him tramp all over the countryside to work it off."

"I can't believe how much the English love to walk," Garrett added. "Puts us car-dependent folks to shame."

"Ask him about the fishing in Scotland," Samantha said. "I know he's dying to tell you."

"Salmon this big." Garrett released Samantha to place his hands two and a half feet apart.

Click.

All three turned in the direction of the sound.

Chloe lowered the camera to extend her hand. "Hi. I'm Chloe Atherton. The reporter from the *Sun*." At Samantha's questioning frown, she added, "Sheriff McQuire and I agreed to a special report on his department. I've been following Mack…Deputy Whittaker this past week."

Slowly, trying—unsuccessfully—not to grin, Garrett turned to Mack. "How's that been working out?"

Mack felt the color drain from his face.

Sudden understanding flickered in Garrett's eyes. And right then and there Mack vowed never to discuss women with his old buddy ever again.

"There's a report on your desk," Mack said.

"Come on," Garrett said, wheedling him. "Fill me in."

Samantha shook her husband's arm. "No shoptalk! We're here to mix and mingle. Socially."

Rory wove his way to them through the crowd. "Hey, y'all, I'm starving. But Miss June won't let me have so much as a sniff before you two have filled a plate."

"Then we must fill a plate," Samantha said, pulling her stepson into a hug. "We can't have that hollow leg collapsing."

As Samantha and Rory, arm in arm, turned toward the refreshment table, Garrett stepped protectively between his family and Chloe. "Ms. Atherton," he said. "I hope you have enough photos of us."

"Of course," she replied with an understanding nod.

"Good." Garrett punched Mack on the shoulder. "Then stay here and take all the shots you want of this handsome—did anyone say *single?*—deputy."

Chloe watched the two men with interest, but after Garrett left to follow his wife and son, she began loading her camera into her backpack.

Mack could identify with her reluctance to talk to him.

"I need to relieve Rollins and Darden back at headquarters," he said at last, trying to extricate himself from the possibility of a goodbye.

"And I need to get back to Brevard." She zipped her backpack with a flourish. "The Yugo's all packed."

"God, I hate thinking of you driving these mountainous roads in that thing." He nearly bit his tongue in surprise at the proprietary tone. Who'd said that?

Chloe blushed and the moment stretched awkwardly.

"Remember the *team* when you write the article," he cautioned.

"Don't you wish," she said with a small smile and a flutter of fingers next to her temple as she turned for the exit. The crowd swallowed her immediately.

Mack headed for headquarters before he found himself admitting what it was he really wished.

CHAPTER FOURTEEN

ENTERING HER BREVARD APARTMENT, Chloe wrinkled her nose. What was that nasty odor?

It didn't take long to discover the week-old, half-empty carton of cottage cheese she'd left on the counter next to the kitchen sink. As a writer, she couldn't think of a more fitting metaphor for her life at present. Curdled. She washed the mess down the garbage disposal, then opened a window and spritzed some air freshener.

Sticking her head in the fridge, she was dismayed to see a yellowing bunch of broccoli, two apples, three limp carrots, a hunk of cheddar, a bag of coffee beans and something fuzzy and green in an open bowl. She grabbed an apple.

With a sigh, she wandered into the living room and surveyed the week's worth of mail she'd brought in and dumped on the ottoman. She glanced at the scattering of leaves her potted plants had dropped on the floor, the knitting supplies she'd bought before this trip but hadn't done anything with—yet had managed to strew the length of her sofa. Her laptop was sending silent accusations from inside her backpack. *When will you get your article written?* it said. At that moment, her life seemed small and circumscribed.

Applegate was maybe a quarter the size of Brevard, but she'd come to feel, if not at home, then more alive there. The citizens had befriended her and pushed her to take a personal inventory.

And Mack?

Besides the fact that he was one hell of a deputy sheriff and subject for an article? Better not go there.

Better start the article. Right now.

Dragging her backpack into her bedroom, she began emptying the contents onto her unmade bed. Her home office. She wished she had one of Sarah Culpepper's hermit bars. Or a couple of June Parker's cranberry-orange scones. Or even a cheeseburger from Phil's Eats. But she bit into the apple as she spread out her copious notes and the tape recorder and its many tapes on the bed linens. When she'd hooked her Nikon up to her computer, she settled back into the pillows to view a slide show of all the photos she'd taken.

Hundreds.

Mostly of Mack.

She deleted the ones where he'd put up his hand to shield his face or had deliberately turned away. But the ones where she'd caught him engrossed in his work took her breath away. Now that she didn't have to worry about appearances, she paused each frame to examine the images of a very compelling man.

Tall, physically fit and serious, he seemed to fill more than her laptop screen. He was there in her bedroom. Only now she couldn't ask him how he got that small bump on an otherwise perfect nose. In unguarded moments his dark brown eyes expressed an inner pain and conflict even as his body exuded authority. One of the shots showed him directing the sandbag filling operation after the storm. His hands drew her into the scene. Strong hands. Lean and long-fingered. Hands that had, if only briefly, claimed possession of her body. She shivered.

How was she going to get through to the other side of this article without injecting personal bias?

How could she turn her experience into a meaningful piece? About a community. About a department. About a man. How could she maintain a journalistic honesty without, as June had put it, rummaging around in someone's pain to sell papers?

And whose pain? His? Or hers?

She glanced at the cell phone among the other items surrounding her on the bed. He'd urged her to phone her parents. And she knew he didn't mean the sort of weekly call to talk about work.

She and Mack had left on neutral terms. There had been no promises to hook up down the road.

Although there hadn't been a grand rift, either, Chloe knew without a doubt there could be no attempt at any kind of relationship until her article was finished.

As her fingers hovered over the keyboard, they shook. She shut her eyes and called up some of what she'd learned. From her mother. *Believe only what you see. What you can prove.*

From Sarah Culpepper. *There's facts and then there's truth.*

Her fingers touched the keys, and she began to write.

STEPPING OUTSIDE THE *Western Carolina Sun* offices Friday at quitting time, Chloe stopped abruptly when she saw a familiar beat-up truck parked at the curb.

Mack—out of uniform—leaned against it.

Hands on hips, legs crossed at the ankle, his body language might be construed as relaxed, but his intense regard was nothing of the sort. She clutched the strap of her ever-protective backpack as trepidation, relief and happiness coursed through her all at once. "Off duty or undercover?" she asked.

"Off duty," he replied, making no effort to explain his presence.

"Then I guess you're not here to arrest me."

"Sounds like a guilty conscience working there."

It was true. They hadn't spoken since Sunday afternoon. Five days. But who was counting? And why should she have called him? She hadn't even called her parents.

When he didn't step away from the pickup, she looked over her shoulder. "Are you waiting for me?"

"Yeah." Appearing uncharacteristically unsure of his next move, however, he hooked his thumbs in his jean pockets and chewed on the inside of his cheek. "I don't know if I should be talking to you now. Have you written your article?"

"It's finished," she said with real pride. Although it hadn't been easy. "At first my editor wanted it to be a series. Then she thought it would pack more punch as a single article, but supersized for Sunday's edition. With all the photos, it takes up most of the Tri-County section." She took a deep breath and added, "I think it's safe to talk to me now."

"I couldn't stay away." He spoke in such a low growl, she wasn't sure she'd heard correctly.

She took a step forward. "I beg your pardon?"

"You heard me." Moving away from his truck to stand right in front of her, he touched her fingertips with his. "I want you," he said so softly she had to lip-read. His eyes said very, very much.

For the past four days, she'd had nothing but tantalizing photos of him, the viewing of which only left her lonely. With a mind of its own, her body leaned toward him. Feeling a huge chunk of her emotional wall crumble, she said, "We are adults."

"Oh, yeah." His crooked grin did her in.

She pointed at her car, parked several spots up the street. "Follow that Yugo."

"Where?"

"To my place."

One eyebrow raised, he looked at her.

"We've determined we're both adults," she declared, her heart racing, "*and* we no longer have a business relationship to maintain."

No sooner had she got the words out of her mouth than he was in his truck. She dashed to her Yugo, then did a U-turn in the middle of the street before leading Mack out of the business district, past the college to the outskirts of town and her small apartment complex. In her haste to park, she ran over the edge of the newly sodded lawn. Let the landscape committee come after her. Leaving her backpack in the Yugo, she grabbed Mack's hand as he sprang from the pickup and pulled him up the outside stairs to her apartment.

Before she could get her key in the lock, Mack hauled her to him and kissed her roughly. There was no ambiguity in this kiss. No deputy holding back.

"Wait!" she said, laughing and sliding down the door to pick up the keys she'd dropped.

"Hey, this was your idea," he claimed as he held her tightly and ran kisses over her neck. Made it next to impossible for her to think, let alone grab the keys.

"And I have to live here." Although most of her neighbors were still at work. And did she care what they thought? Not at the moment. "Aha!" Triumphantly, she held the keys aloft.

Mack was trying to undo her shirt buttons with his teeth.

As she jammed the key in the lock, he turned the knob, and they both tumbled into her apartment. Lying on the floor with Chloe on top, Mack kicked the door closed. "Now what?" he said, laughing.

Mack. Laughing.

The sound made her spirits rise.

"Sex," she breathed. "Hot, middle-of-the-day sex that's nobody's business but our own."

"Where did you learn to talk like that?" he asked as he pulled her closer, a hungry glint in those dark eyes.

"Wouldn't you like to know." There was something emboldening about having him all to herself. Off the clock. One thing was for sure—they were about to alter the feng shui of every room in her apartment. "But first things first."

She hopped up and dashed into her bedroom. Before he had time to do more than roll on his side, head propped on one elbow, and observe her, she grabbed a box of condoms from the drawer of her bedside table, then proceeded to toss several on the bed, then several in the bathroom, several more in the kitchen and the rest in the living room. "Take your pick," she said when she was finished.

He rolled onto his back, his arms and legs thrown out in all directions. "God, she plans to kill me."

And it was a long, slow, exquisite death.

At midnight they finally called for sustenance. Chinese takeout. At 3:00 a.m. they took a bath together. Because he wanted to use the bath crayons a coworker had given her as a gag gift. Mack managed to draw some pretty racy tattoos all over Chloe's body as she covered him in psychedelic flowers. They got laughing so hard, the tenant below pounded on his ceiling. They needed to get out of the bath, anyway, because they'd extinguished all the candles around the tub with their splashing. In the dark they fumbled for towels, and then fell naked into bed.

He entered her with such passion the bed rocked, the headboard banging against the wall. She came before he did, then clung to him as his shoulders heaved and his breath roared in her ears. Her heart thudded against his.

Long minutes they lay together. His weight on her felt like a shield.

And then they slept.

MACK AWOKE TO READ 11:00 A.M. on the bedside clock. He couldn't remember the last time he'd slept so deeply. The sunshine slanting through the blinds revealed Chloe curled against his heart, sleeping with a smile on her face and a smudge of bath crayon still on her shoulder. He felt overwhelmingly tender toward her. She made him feel alive for the first time in a very long while.

For five days he'd battled with himself over whether he should follow her to Brevard. His mother had fairly nagged him to. Garrett and Samantha had both told him he was a fool not to. Hell, the whole town had chimed in on Chloe's departure and what a shame it was. And for that reason, Mack had resisted his own instincts. Desires. Until Sarah Culpepper had groused about cutting off his nose to spite his face. He guessed clichés were clichés for a reason. There was truth to them.

But the tipping point had been the admission aloud in an AA meeting that, unlike his close friends and family, Chloe had discovered every one of his flaws. All his demons.

And she had been remarkably undeterred.

Now he wanted to perform some small, intimate act of appreciation for her. Make breakfast, maybe. Carefully, he got out of bed. Enthralled with her, he bumped the nightstand, and a slew of computer printouts slid to the floor. Her article on the Colum County Sheriff's Department. Titled "The Pulse of a Community."

He had to look.

As he read, his heart sank. He'd braced himself for an exposé. What he got was a testimonial. And he was its object, complete with his personal history and his "acts of generosity." Tanya, Burt, Sarah and Garrett, among others, were interviewed. And all told how Mack had helped them. "Saved them" at one point or another in their lives. Both on and off duty. You'd think nobody else in town did a damned thing.

Sure, the department and its daily activities were written up in detail. Along with other deputies as individuals. But none of them were charging around the article in shining armor on a white steed. Not like this Deputy Whittaker. He didn't recognize the man from Adam.

With great difficulty he stopped himself from tearing the printouts to shreds. But he couldn't hold back the anger. He was pissed that he'd opened up emotionally, that he'd now made a deep physical overture, yet Chloe hadn't seen *him*. Instead, she'd merely processed what she needed. To sell papers.

"What do you think?" she said quietly from behind him.

He turned to look at her, raised slightly on the pillows, her face suffused with contentment. "Do you think this is fair and balanced reporting?" he asked, not caring that his tone was brusque.

"Yes," she said with conviction, sitting up. "With real human interest."

"I thought we agreed I wasn't necessarily a sinner, but I sure wasn't a saint."

"You still can't bring yourself to think you've earned the praise, can you?"

He didn't answer. After reading her supposedly unbiased piece, he couldn't imagine her ever seeing him for who he truly was. Couldn't imagine having a relationship as two human beings, imperfections and all. She'd simply seen the badge and manufactured a hero. To further her career.

"I gotta go," he said.

"Don't," she said, a hitch of panic in her voice. "If you do, you won't come back."

Yeah, she had that right.

He left.

MID-MORNING SUNDAY, MACK was having a devil of a time trying to fix the engine of the family's old and balky tractor when a newspaper landed with a plop on the ground at his feet. He swung around to face the sheriff, who looked as if he'd won the lottery.

Mack wiped his hands on a greasy rag. "Who all has seen that crock?"

"I'd say everyone in town. Except maybe the Baptists. They're still in church. Rachel's Diner is buzzing. I think the newspaper machine in front of Nash's Feed and Seed is sold out."

"And the deputies?"

"They're polishing up a halo for you."

"The article wasn't supposed to go that way. I thought I'd convinced Chloe the department was to be the focus."

"The department looks golden, and its staff looks sterling. Hell, I couldn't have asked for better PR."

"You *like* the article?"

"Why wouldn't I? It's the truth." Garrett looked

him right in the eye. "By the way, I brought your parents an extra copy of the *Sun*. That one—" he pointed to the copy on the ground "—is for your scrapbook. To show your kids."

The guy had the nerve to whistle on his way to the cruiser.

The next few days were no picnic for Mack. People wanted to talk to him. To congratulate him. To clap him on the back. He struggled with their accolades.

It was sixteen months since he'd returned from Iraq. It was ten months since Samantha had found him passed out on her front porch and had hauled him to his first AA meeting. It was only five months since he'd returned to the department full-time. And it was only two and a half weeks since he'd looked into Chloe's soft gray eyes and was forced to confront the man he'd been. The man he was. The man he might become.

It would be nice if he could work through this newfound sense of—what? Belonging?—with Chloe. She'd become the touchstone for working through his feelings.

But he hadn't heard from her.

Filling up his truck at the gas pump, he felt his cell phone vibrate. Every time he hoped against all reason that it would be a Brevard area code. It never was. It wasn't this time. It was Garrett.

"What's up?" he asked as he topped off the tank.

"Some repercussions from Chloe's article."

Damn, would that thing never fade into the sunset?

"I know it's still not your favorite piece of journalism," Garrett said, amusement creeping into his voice. "But someone thinks it's pretty terrific."

Yeah, his mother.

"There's a charitable foundation out of Asheville," Garrett continued. "Families First. As a result of the article, they want to give our department a family-services grant. We'll have the final say as to how it's used."

"That's…great." At least something good had come out of that week.

"They want to make a formal presentation at a ceremony on the courthouse steps this coming Saturday," Garrett continued. "Out in the open. For all to see."

"I'll be there."

"You bet you will be. You and Chloe are going to be the ones accepting the check."

CHAPTER FIFTEEN

FACING THREE NEW OUTFITS laid out on her bed, Chloe was beside herself with apprehension.

As soon as she'd learned that she—and Mack—were to accept the Families First grant check today, she'd gone on an emergency shopping spree. At actual retail stores, not secondhand or vintage boutiques. Looking for clothes that June and Faith might approve of. The presentation was to take place outdoors at one o'clock, Sheriff McQuire had said, so Chloe had chosen three outfits. One if it was seasonably warm and sunny. One if it turned frigid, which it could in the mountains in early May. And one if it rained.

She'd never spent so much on clothing in her life.

And now the day had dawned warm, cloudy and very humid. The weather channel predicted that a storm front was coming through, and behind it temperatures should drop. Great. Why not wear everything she'd bought and adjust the layers as needed throughout the ceremony?

Sheriff McQuire had asked that they all meet up at headquarters at twelve-thirty. She had an hour to get ready and drive to Applegate. One hour before she was to see Mack for the first time since he'd left her.

Apparently his anger over her representation of him in the article overrode any personal connection they'd established.

Did he think he was the only one who'd taken a risk by opening up emotionally?

Exasperated, she said to hell with sartorial indecision and picked one article of clothing from each newly purchased outfit. Let's get this final interaction over with.

WHEN CHLOE STEPPED INTO the sheriff's department offices, it was as if she'd never been away. The deputies on duty stopped to welcome her back. Dispatcher Kim Nash tried to tempt her by opening a container of peanut-butter cookies.

"No, thank you," Chloe said, waving it away. "Where's the sheriff?"

"He and Whittaker are in one of the cells," Kim replied. "Looking for who knows what. The sheriff said for you to go on back."

"Cells?" She didn't remember any prisoners housed here.

"Before the detention center was built, the only lockup was in this building. Now the old jail's used for storage." Kim pointed toward the back. "Hang a right by the meeting room and follow the musty odor."

She didn't need to follow the odor. She was led by the sound of Mack's and Sheriff McQuire's heated discussion.

"It's obviously not back here," Mack said, his voice full of irritation.

"It is. Keep looking," Garrett replied.

"What makes you think we even *have* one?"

"June said she remembered it being presented to some senator back in the eighties."

"Terrific. Twenty years ago. Besides, if it was presented to the senator, wouldn't he or she have it?"

"It was a symbolic presentation."

"And what would make you want to dig it out now? Ow!" Mack's complaint devolved into a series of mumbled curses.

"I thought it would be a nice gesture." There was something—veiled amusement?—in the sheriff's tone that didn't translate as wholly official.

"It's unnecessarily corny," Mack groused.

"Hi," Chloe said, coming upon a junk-filled cell and the two lawmen. One exasperated, and one, yes, obviously amused. "Kim said I'd find you here."

"Hey!" Garrett spread his arms in welcome, a broad smile on his face. Mack continued his diligent search for what he'd seconds ago dismissed as unnecessarily corny. "Come on in," the sheriff urged. "Maybe you have better eyes than we do."

Mack sucked in his breath and beetled his brows as if he thought the sheriff had gone bonkers.

"What are you searching for?" Chloe asked, squeezing into the cell.

"A ceremonial key to the town," Mack muttered.

Garrett's walkie-talkie went off. Loud and clear, Kim's voice rang out. "Did Chloe find her way back there?"

"She did."

"Then you have a phone call."

"Excuse me," the sheriff said, brushing past Chloe and stepping into the hallway. "You two keep looking."

"I don't think we need to stay back here," Mack said. "To search for a damned—"

"I think you do." Garrett slammed the cell door shut with a startling clang, locked it and pocketed the key with a dramatic flourish.

"McQuire!" Mack roared, knocking over a stack of boxes as he charged the door. "What do you think you're doing?"

"Giving you two some time to work out your differences."

"This is ridiculous!" In a panic Chloe grabbed the cold metal bars. "How long do you intend to keep us here?"

"As long as necessary." The sheriff looked at his watch. "The Families First presentation is scheduled to start in twenty-five minutes. But it won't happen without you. Now you could choose to hold up those good folks, but I'm counting on the altruism I've observed in both of you to broker some kind of meeting of the minds before one."

He turned on his heel and left Chloe and Mack locked together.

Amid shoulder-high stacks of boxes and the smell of old cardboard, Chloe suddenly experienced the beginnings of claustrophobia. When McQuire had been in the cell, there'd been barely enough room for the three of them to stand still. Now, with two, the space seemed even smaller. All this paper and not a brown bag to breathe into.

"I don't know what he expects," Mack said, his back to her.

"He expects us to make peace." Chloe leaned against the bars and sighed. She was none too optimistic about the prospect.

Mack turned to face her. There was longing in his eyes. "No. I think he expects more than that."

She'd fallen for that look once before. And what had it gotten her? Great sex, yeah, but heartache afterward.

Lacking paper-bag therapy, she exhaled sharply several times in a row. "It appears you haven't been run out of town because of my article," she said at last, trying for light. Trying for adult. Trying to pretend Mack hadn't meant more to her than a passing physical attraction.

"No," he replied. "I'm still on the force. But sadly,

I think we're scheduled to segue right from the grant presentation to canonization."

She fought back a smile. "Tell me that the article wasn't a mistake."

"Okay, the article wasn't a mistake." The hitch in his voice told her the admission cost him. "The grant will be able to help people like Tanya Donahue and her kids more consistently than I ever could on my own."

"Allowing you to see Tanya and the others as friends and family rather than penance?"

He flinched. "Low blow, but one I deserve."

"Do you mean that, or are you using your get-out-of-jail-free card?"

His laugh sounded more like a hoarse bark. "I don't know why, but I've missed your constant probing."

"Well, I'm angry at you, Whittaker. You left me."

He stooped to pick up the boxes he'd tipped over. "You told me not to come back."

"Uh-uh." She poked his shoulder. Waited until he stood up and faced her. "I *said* if you left, you *wouldn't* come back. I knew if you couldn't stay and work out our differences of opinion, there wasn't much hope for us."

"I don't think it's a simple matter of differences of opinion. We see the world differently. You think full disclosure. I think, hey, let's maintain some privacy."

"No. I think let's communicate. Let's get the facts on the table. Let's look the truth square in the eye. You think walls."

"Is that what you want in a relationship? Full disclosure?"

"Communication. Yes. Definitely."

When he caught her eye, his expression was full of doubt. "Did you ever call your parents?"

Chloe took a step backward. Because of the frank talk Mack and she had had in June's B and B, Chloe had eventually built up enough courage to phone her parents. To talk about Claire. To apologize for distancing herself from the two people she loved fiercely.

"Chloe?" Her name on Mack's lips startled her.

"I did call them."

All irritation seemed to drain from his body. He reached out to touch her arm. "How did that work out?"

"It was painful." She twisted the hammered-silver ring on her finger. "Athertons aren't the touchy-feely sort." She fought back tears to look at him. "But you were right. It was necessary." Puzzled by his forbidding expression, she asked, "What's wrong?"

"Not so much wrong, as earth-shattering." He began to pace the cramped quarters. "Here I hated your article, but it turned out great for the community. You didn't want to make that phone call, but because of it, you might have a shot at being happy."

When his pacing began to drive her nuts, she put out a hand to stop him. "What are you trying to say?"

"I don't know, Atherton. Maybe we work better as a team. What do you say?"

"Frankly I don't know," she replied, suddenly feeling very warm and wondering if she should peel off a layer of her new outfit. "I've pretty much kept people at arm's length in the past." Looking away from him, she ran a finger along the crossbar of the cell door and came up with a ski-cap of dust. She shook it off. "And that didn't work out. So I'm open to new suggestions."

There was a long, awkward pause before Mack said, "I'm not perfect."

"Boy, do I know that." Inappropriate laughter welled up inside her, and she cleared her throat several times to regain her self-control. "If I even considered partnering with you, I'd have to expect nothing less than a roller-coaster ride."

"Look at me, please," he said softly.

She did and saw that he seemed to be struggling for self-control, too.

"You're not perfect yourself," he said. "I'd have to worry when I brush my teeth if it's going to make the next day's paper."

"Get over yourself, Whittaker. You're yesterday's news." Although, as he stood in front of her, broad-chested in that perfectly pressed uniform, his eyes flashing, Chloe doubted that he or his story would ever grow old to her.

"And I'm glad to be out of the limelight," he said. "Do you think now we could…?"

"Could what?"

"You know."

She stepped forward to slip her arms around his waist. "The only *you know* that I know has taken place between us shouldn't take place again in a former jail-cell-turned-closet."

"I recognize this tactic, Atherton." He slipped his arms around her shoulders. "You're forcing me to communicate."

"Mmm-hmm." She was beginning to like the new semi-cooperative Mack. "And call me Chloe."

"Do you think now we could see each other?" he asked, gazing down at her.

"I won't consider it unless you answer one more question." She felt his muscles tense beneath her fingertips.

"Yes?" There was warning in the one syllable.

"How did you break your nose?"

"Football." Okay, so the new openness hadn't necessarily made him an orator. "Now, answer my question. Can we see each other? Seriously."

"I hope not too seriously," she replied, laying her cheek against his chest. Relishing the steady beat of his heart. "I found a place online to buy bath crayons by the case."

He tipped her chin upward, then lowered his mouth to hers and told her everything he hadn't put into words.

Behind them, someone cleared his throat. Chloe and Mack broke apart to find Sheriff McQuire outside the cell, examining his watch. "Sixteen minutes, four seconds to a resolution. There's hope for you two."

There was more than hope. Call it reporter's intuition, but Chloe felt that here was the potential for a lifelong challenge. And she wouldn't have to remain objective.

EPILOGUE

RACHEL SLID TWO SERVINGS of gooseberry pie onto the diner table.

"Hey, Whittaker," Breckinridge said on her way out the door. "I'm glad to see you signed up for the fall softball league. With our lousy record, we could use an ace."

Chloe squeezed Mack's fingers. "*You* signed up for a softball league? How social."

"Yeah, well, some people think I've found a good influence. I'd like to talk about that."

Tanya burst into the diner and made a beeline for their table. "I have the best news, y'all," she said as she slid into the booth next to Chloe. "I've come from the board of education offices, and this year I'm going to be a classroom aide in Pete and Emma's school. We can all ride together, and we'll have the same hours and same vacations. And my sister says she'll babysit Wayans."

"That's terrific!" Chloe exclaimed.

Mack noticed how, now that he didn't see Tanya

as part of some necessary atonement for Nate's death, he could sit back and relish her growing happiness. As a friend.

That friend looked under the table. "Oops, I kicked your backpack over, Chloe." She reached down to right it, but came up with a pair of pink, hand-crocheted baby booties. "What have we here?" she asked, dangling the yarnwork high above the table and glancing first at Chloe, then at Mack.

Mack began to do some backwards math.

"These?" Chloe replied, calmly retrieving them from Tanya. "I'm going to do a human-interest story on Kate Ingalls up in Beecham's Hollow. Without any kind of fanfare, she crochets booties, caps, sweaters and blankets for babies in orphanages. From North Carolina to halfway around the world."

Mack felt unaccountably disappointed.

Tanya got up to spread her job news to Rachel and the other diner patrons.

"Are you okay?" Chloe asked.

He fingered one of the tiny booties. "Do you see kids anywhere in your future?"

"After playing Wii with Rory, I'm beginning to. But I'm still not sure of them when they're the size of Pete and Emma and Wayans. Do you suppose I could start with a teenager and work backwards?"

"I have an idea. What if we babysit Tanya's kids for an evening? Let her go out to celebrate her new job."

"Hey, are you pushing this baby idea?"

After Iraq, he'd doubted he'd ever again entertain the idea. He hadn't wanted to bring a child or children into a world that could be so capricious. But in the past few months…

"Not so much pushing as offering a bit of experimentation," he said softly, trying to keep their conversation private. "But first there's something I haven't told you."

Shadows clouded her beautiful gray eyes, and he couldn't stand to make her worry for even a second. "I love you," he said, low, so only she could hear. Although he'd felt it for some time now, he'd never told her.

"Wow." Her face had the look of someone who'd received the best Christmas present ever. "You know…I love you."

How could he not feel it?

He took her hand and curled the bootie into it. "I realize there are a few steps between 'I love you' and rug rats."

"I have time." She smiled that smile that made him believe the world was a decent place. "And you know me. I don't give up on a project once I've taken it on."

Didn't he know it. And why did he ever think that was a bad thing?

"So does Kate want this pair of booties back?" he asked.

"No. Surprisingly, she told me to keep them."

No surprise. Some things were meant to be.

Mack felt himself taking that first emotional step beyond *I love you*.

Love Inspired
HISTORICAL

*Powerful, engaging stories of romance,
adventure and faith set in the past—
when life was simpler and faith played a
major role in everyday lives.*

See below for a sneak preview of
HIGH COUNTRY BRIDE
by Jillian Hart

Love Inspired Historical—
love and faith throughout the ages

Silence remained between them, and she felt the rake of his gaze, taking her in from the top of her wind-blown hair where escaped tendrils snapped in the wind to the toe of her scuffed, patched shoes. She watched him fist up his big, work-roughened hands and expected the worst.

"You never told me, Miz Nelson. Where are you going to go?" His tone was flat, his jaw tensed as if he were still fighting his temper. His blue gaze shot past her to watch the children going about their picking up.

"I don't know." Her throat went dry. Her tongue felt thick as she answered. "When I find employment, I could wire a payment to you. Rent. Y-you aren't think-ing of bringing the sher-rif in?"

"You think I want *payment?*" He boomed like winter thunder. *"You think I want rent money?"*

"Frankly, I don't know what you want."

"I'll tell you what I don't want. I don't want—" His words cannoned in the silence as he paused, and a passing pair of geese overhead honked in flat-noted tones. He grimaced, and it was impossible to know what he would say or do.

She trembled, not from fear of him, she truly didn't believe he would strike her, but from the unknown. Of being forced to take the frightening step off the only safe spot she'd known since she'd lost Pa's house.

When you were homeless, everything seemed so fragile, so easily off balance, for it was a big, unkind world for a woman alone with her children. She had no one to protect her. No one to care. The truth was, she'd never had those things in her husband. How could she expect them from any stranger? Especially this man she hardly knew, who was harsh and cold and hard-hearted.

And, worse, what if he brought in the law?

"You can't keep living out of a wagon," he said, still angry, the cords still straining in his neck. "Animals have enough sense to keep their young cared for and safe."

Yes, it was as she'd thought. He intended to be as cruel about this as he could be. She spun on her heel, pulling up all her defenses, and was determined to let his upcoming hurtful words roll off her like rainwater on an oiled tarp. She grabbed the towel the children had neatly folded and tossed it into the laundry box in the back of the wagon.

"Miz Nelson. I'm talking to you."

"Yes, I know. If you expect me to stand there while you tongue lash me, you're mistaken. I have packing to get to." Her fingers were clumsy as she hefted the bucket of water she'd brought for washing—she wouldn't need that now—and heaved.

His hand clasped on the handle beside hers, and she could feel the life and power of him vibrate along the thin metal. "Give it to me."

Her fingers let go. She felt stunned as he walked away, easily carrying the bucket that had been so heavy to her, and quietly, methodically, put out the small cooking fire. He did not seem as ominous or as intimidating—somehow—as he stood in the shadows, bent to his task, although she couldn't say why that was. Perhaps it was because he wasn't acting the way she was used to men acting. She was quite used to doing all the work.

Jamie scurried over, juggling his wooden horses, to watch. Daisy hung back, eyes wide and still, taking in the mysterious goings-on.

He is different when he's near to them, she realized. He didn't seem harsh, and there was no hint of anger—or, come to think of it, any other emotion—as he shook out the empty bucket, nodded once to the children and then retraced his path to her.

"Let me guess." He dropped the bucket onto the tailgate, and his anger appeared to be back. Cords strained in his neck and jaw as he growled at her. "If you leave here, you don't know where you're going and you have no money to get there with?"

She nodded. "Yes, sir."

"Then get you and your kids into the wagon. I'll hitch up your horses for you." His eyes were cold and yet they were not unfeeling as he fastened his gaze on hers. "I have an empty shanty out back of my house that no one's living in. You can stay there for the night."

"What?" She stumbled back, and the solid wood of the tailgate bit into the small of her back. "But—"

"There will be no argument," he bit out, interrupting her. "None at all. I buried a wife and son years ago, what was most precious to me, and to see you and them neglected like this—with no one to care—" His jaw ground again and his eyes were no longer cold.

Joanna didn't think she'd ever seen anything sadder than Aiden McKaslin as the sun went down on him.

* * * * *

Don't miss this deeply moving story,
HIGH COUNTRY BRIDE,
available July 2008
from the new Love Inspired Historical line.

Also look for SEASIDE CINDERELLA
by Anna Schmidt,
where a poor servant girl and a
wealthy merchant prince
might somehow make a life together.

REQUEST YOUR FREE BOOKS!
2 FREE NOVELS PLUS 2 FREE GIFTS!

HARLEQUIN®

Super Romance®

Exciting, emotional, unexpected!

YES! Please send me 2 FREE Harlequin Superromance® novels and my 2 FREE gifts (gifts are worth about $10). After receiving them, if I don't wish to receive any more books, I can return the shipping statement marked "cancel." If I don't cancel, I will receive 6 brand-new novels every month and be billed just $4.69 per book in the U.S. or $5.24 per book in Canada, plus 25¢ shipping and handling per book and applicable taxes, if any*. That's a savings of close to 15% off the cover price! I understand that accepting the 2 free books and gifts places me under no obligation to buy anything. I can always return a shipment and cancel at any time. Even if I never buy another book from Harlequin, the two free books and gifts are mine to keep forever.

135 HDN EEX7 336 HDN EEYK

Name	(PLEASE PRINT)	
Address		Apt. #
City	State/Prov.	Zip/Postal Code

Signature (if under 18, a parent or guardian must sign)

Mail to the **Harlequin Reader Service:**
IN U.S.A.: P.O. Box 1867, Buffalo, NY 14240-1867
IN CANADA: P.O. Box 609, Fort Erie, Ontario L2A 5X3

Not valid to current subscribers of Harlequin Superromance books.

Want to try two free books from another line?
Call 1-800-873-8635 or visit www.morefreebooks.com.

* Terms and prices subject to change without notice. N.Y. residents add applicable sales tax. Canadian residents will be charged applicable provincial taxes and GST. Offer not valid in Quebec. This offer is limited to one order per household. All orders subject to approval. Credit or debit balances in a customer's account(s) may be offset by any other outstanding balance owed by or to the customer. Please allow 4 to 6 weeks for delivery. Offer available while quantities last.

Your Privacy: Harlequin is committed to protecting your privacy. Our Privacy Policy is available online at www.eHarlequin.com or upon request from the Reader Service. From time to time we make our lists of customers available to reputable third parties who may have a product or service of interest to you. If you would prefer we not share your name and address, please check here. ☐

HSR08R

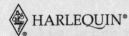

HARLEQUIN®

American ★ Romance®

DOUBLE THE REASONS
TO PARTY!

**We are celebrating American Romance's
25th Anniversary just in time to make
your Fourth of July celebrations
sensational with Kraft!**

KRAFT

American Romance is presenting
four fabulous recipes from Kraft,
to make sure your Fourth of July
celebrations are a hit! Each
American Romance book in June contains a different
recipe—a salad, appetizer, main course or a dessert.
Collect all four in June wherever books are sold!

kraftfoods.com—
deliciously simple. everyday.

Or visit kraftcanada.com
for more delicious meal ideas.

www.eHarlequin.com   KRAFTBPA

SAVE $1.00

A riveting trilogy from

BRENDA NOVAK

SAVE $1.00 on the purchase price of one book in The Last Stand trilogy from Brenda Novak.

Offer valid from May 27, 2008, to August 30, 2008.
Redeemable at participating retail outlets. Limit one coupon per purchase.

HARLEQUIN®

Super Romance®

COMING NEXT MONTH

#1500 TRUSTING RYAN • Tara Taylor Quinn

For Detective Ryan Mercedes, right and wrong are clear. And what he feels for guardian ad litem Audrey Lincoln is very right. Their shared pursuit of justice proves they're on the same side. But when a case divides them, can he see things her way?

#1501 A MARRIAGE BETWEEN FRIENDS • Melinda Curtis
Marriage of Inconvenience

They were friends who married when Jill needed a father for her unborn child, and Vince offered his name. Then, unexpectedly, Jill walked out. Now, eleven years later, Vince Patrizio is back to reclaim his wife…and the son who should have been theirs.

#1502 HIS SON'S TEACHER • Kay Stockham
The Tulanes of Tennessee

Nick Tulane has never fallen for a teacher. A former dropout, he doesn't go for the academic type. Until he meets Jennifer Rose, that is. While she's busy helping his son catch up at school, Nick starts wishing for some private study time with the tutor.

#1503 THE CHILD COMES FIRST • Elizabeth Ashtree

Star defense attorney Simon Montgomery is called upon to defend a girl who claims to be wrongly accused of murder. Her social worker Jayda Kavanagh believes she's innocent. But as Simon and Jayda grow close trying to save the child, Jayda's own youthful trauma could stand between her and the love Simon offers.

#1504 NOBODY'S HERO • Carrie Alexander
Count on a Cop

Massachusetts state police officer Sean Rafferty has sworn off ever playing hero again. All he wants is to be left alone to recover. Which is perfect, because Connie Bradford doesn't need a hero in her life. Unfortunately, her grieving daughter does…

#1505 THE WAY HOME • Jean Brashear
Everlasting Love

They'd been everything to each other. But Bella Parker—stricken with amnesia far from home—can't remember any of it…not even the betrayal that made her leave. Now James Parker has to decide how much of their past he should tell her. Because the one piece that could jog her memory might destroy them forever.

HSRCNM0608